DAVID AND THE GIANT

by ~~Michael~~ Callahan

December 2008

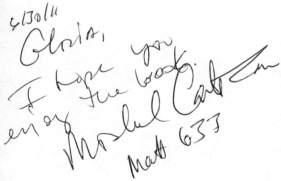

INFINITY
PUBLISHING

All rights reserved. No part of this book shall be reproduced or transmitted in any form or by any means, electronic, mechanical, magnetic, photographic including photocopying, recording or by any information storage and retrieval system, without prior written permission of the publisher. No patent liability is assumed with respect to the use of the information contained herein. Although every precaution has been taken in the preparation of this book, the publisher and author assume no responsibility for errors or omissions. Neither is any liability assumed for damages resulting from the use of the information contained herein.

Copyright © 2011 by Michael Callahan

Editor: Cathy Kessler
Photography and Graphic Design: Johnny Parisi
Graphic Creation and Layout Production: Kristin M. Quackenbush "Q"

ISBN 0-7414-6350-4

Printed in the United States of America

This is a work of fiction. Names, characters, places, and incidents either are the product of the author's imagination or are used fictitiously. Any resemblance to actual events or locales or persons, living or dead, is entirely coincidental.

Published January 2011

INFINITY PUBLISHING
1094 New DeHaven Street, Suite 100
West Conshohocken, PA 19428-2713
Toll-free (877) BUY BOOK
Local Phone (610) 941-9999
Fax (610) 941-9959
Info@buybooksontheweb.com
www.buybooksontheweb.com

Acknowledgments

I would like to thank my wife, Libby, for being patient with me during the two years to write this book and for supporting my dreams and goals in life. Also, I want to thank my mother for encouraging me.

Contents

1: Ray and His Childhood 1
2: Ray's Interests, Ideas, and Training 7
3: The Development of the Mikecrodent Chip 12
4: The BBB Interference 28
5: Ray's Faith 31
6: Ray's Family 37
7: A Typical Day at the Office 42
8: Medical-Dental Mission Trips 50
9: The Twin Towers' Attacks 53
10: The Koran and the Muslim Radicals 56
11: Bin Laden, al-Qaeda, and the Taliban 60
12: Ray Reveals the Mega Experience 65
13: The Abduction 74
14: Relocation 81
15: Meeting the Giant 86
16: The Day after the Dental Evaluation 96
17: The Big Idea 99
18: The Bizarre Surgery 101
19: The Rescue 112
20: The Location and Capture of bin Laden 116
21: Meeting the President 123
22: The Conclusion 125

PROLOGUE

David and the Giant is the story of a dentist and his wife who set out on an adventure to the Middle East, a mission trip to provide dental and medical care to the Iraqi refugees who were coming into Jordan in order to flee the régime of Saddam Hussein. As the couple tours the countryside for a pleasure travel break from their fatigue of clinic, they encounter a most shocking and life-threatening experience. As captives in a foreign land, they are forced to treat a patient whose name is known around the world. Since September 11, 2001, he has been the most wanted man on Earth. They must endure hunger, thirst, and filthy living conditions. Held captive, blindfolded, and terrorized, they are required to perform one of the most bizarre and amazing surgeries in dentistry documented to date.

This moving story parallels the Biblical one with a similar prophecy. When Ray realizes that he has taken on the role of King David and his patient is the "Giant," he chooses the only stone in his sling, a device that Ray has developed and patented. The story delineates Ray's faith to survive and conquer, as he comes face to face with the giant up close and then takes the giant down. Ray's desire to change the world and make it a better place is finally achieved.

~ 1 ~

Ray and His Childhood

My life has been one of searching for answers. I grew up experiencing some of the cruelties that life has to offer and hardships that come with it. See, most of my early life has been formed from the inspiration of my beloved sister who was abducted and never found. Since my sister's absence, I have become more and more fixated on making the wrongs of this world right, trying to make it somewhat of a better place for the living.

More recently, I have practiced dentistry for the last part of 20 years, which has been a purposeful occupation and has led me to an era in my life that will be forever changed. I believe I am a man called for a special assignment, one who searches for answers to the past in order to protect innocent people like my sister, Carla. I guess you could say that's why I am in the predicament that I am in now.

I'm struggling for my life surrounded by insurgents who are vowing to destroy me because of who I am and the information I hold within me. Cavebound and desperate to make it back into the safety of my own country, I'm wary that may never become reality.

As my wife, Trudy, and I cuddled closely together in the underground cave, I began to think back on my life as it had been in childhood. I had heard that people do this before they die, and this appeared to be the appropriate time. I was trying hard to keep my faith, but the reality of what was happening was overwhelming. However, when I thought of being with Carla, my little sister, calmness swept over me, and I found myself smiling. That is, until the horror of what happened to her swept through my mind. Each time I closed my eyes, it would all come back to me.

My name is Ray, and I was born in Athens, Georgia, in 1961. Being somewhat confident at the time, I felt like I was a fine-looking twelve-year-old boy, fast on my feet and a good personality, or so I was told. I probably inherited some of my better gifts from my parents who loved me unconditionally and assured me often that I could be anything I wanted to be—if I had determination. My mother read to me, usually books that had educational value. She worked at the local telephone company, and my father, who was a good, hard-working man, was highly skilled in the high-tech computer-robotic field. The long drive to and from a military facility in Atlanta did not take time away from his family.

A big part of my life was my little sister, Carla. At age 11, being a big brother to a five-year-old can be tiring at times, but I saw it as being adult enough to be responsible. Truthfully, at times it was nice to be able to tell someone to do or not to do something. We seldom fought except when Mom made a chocolate cake and the decision had to be made as to who got to lick the bowl. After Mom had cleaned the dishes, the next thing would be to help save Carla's life when she climbed up on the high countertop to put the bowl on the top shelf. I think I remember feeling very big and important, as I reminded her of what could happen if I were not there to catch her if she fell. Carla adored me and promised not to climb ever again if I would tell one of her favorite imaginative stories about a princess that lived in a distant, cold, and dangerous land.

Most of my friends did not understand the love I had for my younger sister. They reminded me that it wasn't cool and that you were supposed to hate spending time with your sister. Well, Carla came along late in life for Mom, and she was a tremendous surprise for them as well as for me. Truthfully, I was glad Carla turned out to be a girl. I had a sibling, yet, still, I was the only boy in the family. It felt as though I had some authority or responsibility toward my baby sister.

As Carla grew, nighttime was story time for her, and who do you suppose she wanted to read or tell the story? Me, of course. It was a perfect opportunity for me to daydream and tell her how I visualized my future and how I wanted to be the one who made a difference in this world. I would tell Carla that she could make the world better too and that she can change the world. Carla's eyes would become big; she wanted to hear more and more of my story. Perhaps it was then that I began to see that, like Mom said, "Ray, you can do anything you want to do." The years went by quickly, and I began to see myself as someone who could realistically make a difference. Little did I know that it would take a tragedy for me to conquer THE GIANT IN MY LIFE.

Carla could hardly wait for the ice-cream man to come around each day, honking that funny horn and causing excitement within hearing distance of the familiar sound. Mom or Dad usually left ice-cream money for the two of us. I always stayed with Carla for fear she might become excited and run into the street. Today was Tuesday: my day to take care of her for the extra hour that Mom had to work. Taking care of my little sister was not hard for me, as I took on the role of "big brother" and made Mom and Dad proud of me.

On this particular day, I was totally in awe of a magazine article I started reading called "Science and the Beautiful Balance of Symmetry." Dad had explained enough about the meaning of the article to get me interested. Meanwhile, as I read, I watched Carla patiently sitting on a bench waiting for the ice-cream truck. She had her usual toys with her, her wagonful of dolls and their baby bottles. She said if she were going to have ice cream, her babies would need something too. Then she went on to explain to them that her favorite ice cream was a strawberry cone wrapped in nuts, but that they would have to grow and get big before they could have that. I never tired of hearing her talk, always using her imagination.

However, this day I could hear her talking but not clearly. As I leaned back in the porch swing stretching and reflecting on what I had just read, for a moment, only a moment, I closed my eyes. Suddenly the quietness alerted me to something. Not really knowing what, I realized Carla was not on the bench, nor had I heard the ice-cream truck. I thought, *How impossible when just seconds ago she was there!*

Much like a crazy person, I found myself running in every direction screaming Carla's name. So many things were running through my head. I was watching her—*was I watching her?* Was she playing a hiding game with me and what do I do now? I looked around to question the other children that usually played in the area nearby, but no one was there. Where was the ice-cream man? Had I been so deeply into what I was reading that I missed all of this? I prayed, "God, please help find Carla."

Suddenly Mom appeared, and I had the horrible task of telling her what happened. After we decided that someone must have taken our precious little Carla, totally devastated, we called the police and my father. The police investigators found Carla's favorite doll on the ground beside her wagon. The investigators assured us that everything possible was being done and we would be notified and updated shortly. "Shortly" turned into days with no calls or updates, so we would call the authorities to try and get information. It seemed they weren't working fast enough and not as interested as they should have been. My parents had posters printed with Carla's picture on it and asked people to call our number if they had any information of her whereabouts. Friends told us that our sorrow and pain made it just seem as though the authorities weren't taking a great interest in my sister's case. Yes, we were hurting, but that's what any caring parent would feel. We wanted her found today. Today never came.

To this day, Carla was never found. How could our lives go on? Friends from our church, Carla's school, and everywhere surrounded us with love, encouragement, and hope, but nothing could ease my grief or that of my parents. The worst part of it all was that I blamed myself and would live with that for the rest of my life.

Friends reminded us that life must go on, and it did. However, quite differently. Mom and Dad went to work every day, and we all went to church on Sunday. I went to school and again played baseball and basketball. Going home each day was extremely hard because Carla wasn't there pulling on my shirt, begging me to play with her or read her a story.

My family continued to live in Athens. We found ourselves suspiciously looking at everyone we saw at large gatherings, silently asking, *"Did you take our Carla?"* Our friends and family were so helpful. They all tried to keep us busy and involved in something. That was good but sometimes interfered with my plans.

Being thirteen wasn't a bad age for me. I wasn't treated like a baby, and sometimes I was allowed to go places with my two best friends, Trey and Richard. Like most young boys, we were always trying to come up with a new game or just something exciting to do. I think our most thrilling entertainment was to see who could swim across our backyard river the fastest. It was twenty feet wide and very swift, which made the challenge for us even greater. If only Mom and Dad had known of this dangerous play, but, thankfully, they didn't.

Life had become somewhat bearable, and at fourteen, I was enjoying most sports. One day during math class, I noticed several of the students being asked to leave the room. After a few minutes, several more left the room, and as soon as they returned, my name and some others were called. I was told that the school was examining each student for scoliosis. That did not bother me at all because I knew I was all right even though I didn't even know what scoliosis was.

But then my parents received a letter from the school saying that I may have scoliosis and should be seen by a physician. A doctor in Atlanta, who was experienced in this area, was recommended to us. After seeing this doctor and being told that I would have to wear a back brace, which would fit around my waist and up to my neck, I just sat there in disbelief. I was told that I would have to wear this brace to school (for everyone to stare at) and no sports for two years! No, I just couldn't do it! The doctor very firmly informed me that I would be crippled if I did not wear the brace, so that was quickly settled. Yes, I would have to wear this uncomfortable appliance to prevent the curve in my spine from getting worse, but I hated it. Other kids pointed at me, stared, and were afraid to walk up to me and ask what happened.

As these things occurred, I struggled with rejection and exclusion from society, mainly my peers. I deliberately became withdrawn from these seemingly uncaring people and immersed myself in the sciences and creative arts. As time passed, I would discover that my introverted behavior could be an obstacle, keeping me from my purpose and destiny. Dad encouraged me to change my attitude and reconnect with people, in spite of my physical problems. He also said that I should use this time as an adventure, thinking about what I might want to do in the future. It was for certain that I had plenty of time to think. Yes, the idea was a good one. I needed to focus on my future and not on this moment!

~ 2 ~
Ray's Interests, Ideas, and Training

In my late teenage years, I began to appreciate music, art, and collecting Indian relics. I often would write, compose, and record music with lyrics. I would sing the lyrics and record the music for my own pleasure. I really couldn't sing that well, but that didn't stop me from enjoying music. My artwork included plaster moldings of abstract shapes with geometric formations. I once took a large tree leaf that was a foot in diameter and imprinted the image and texture with its shape onto wet soft plaster and then shaped images on each side. I then contoured copper piping around the piece, in the shape of a teardrop. I was very proud of this creative piece and hung it up over my fireplace mantle in my home later.

There was a period of time in my life when I became interested in words and the power they held. I marveled at the meaning of specific words. Words like love, sincerity, vision, purpose, destiny, leadership, real, communicate, kindness, peace, kingdom, eternal, life, and light were at the top of my list. This interest in words led me further into expressing my thoughts and stories on paper. I began writing literary books for children that told stories that had meaning to help them learn concepts and values.

I gradually became a people person and enjoyed being around people who were genuine and showed kindness to others. It especially pleased me to see young people grow to be strong and wise in life. I once grew my hair long and donated ten inches to the "Locks of Love" organization for children who had cancer and had lost their hair. The hair locks were used to make wigs for the children during their chemotherapy stage of treatment.

During the two years it took me to grow my hair the required ten inches for "Locks of Love" for a child with cancer, I learned a thing or two. I found that, oftentimes, people would give me strange looks at the grocery store and at some of the community meetings I attended. It seemed that some people were prejudice toward me and saw me as a rebel. This bothered me at first, and then I decided that it was okay. I have always believed in myself and felt I didn't have to justify my actions to anyone but God. I knew that God was okay with my long hair.

I thought that if people were going to label me as such, then I should have the freedom to go further and be even freer. So I came home one day riding on my brand-new Harley-Davidson Sportster motorcycle. I thought it went well with my long hair. Maybe I was indeed a rebel. One of the bikers I rode with at that time told me that I needed to consider tattoos, but tattoos were not on my things-to-do list. I enjoyed my bike and would take off and ride the highways with a sense of freedom and release.

One day, I was riding in the mountains and stopped in a small town in Tennessee. I saw a man who had several tattoos outside a small fast-food place. At first glance, he looked like a man who was dangerous and untrustworthy. As I went to get back onto my bike, the man came running up to me. It startled me at first since I didn't know what he wanted. I soon discovered that he was trying to tell me that my wallet had fallen out of my pocket on the ground when I was getting on my motorcycle. The man reached down and picked up my wallet and handed it to me and smiled. I was pleasantly surprised and said, "Thank you!" As I left the parking lot, I thought to myself, *I hope I never prejudge anyone again. I hope I always give people the benefit of the doubt and think the best of everyone.*

As time passed, I grew increasingly obsessed with all forms of science, especially biotechnology and technology with human interfaces. As I researched the fascination of science, I discovered that I wanted to become an entrepreneur dentist and change the world in the advancements of dental science. Mr. Webe, my high-school advisor, had rejected my dreams of dental science, due to my physical condition. He thought that my back condition would limit my abilities in dentistry since dentists lean over the patient for hours at a time and this could fatigue the back. I couldn't believe that others, including my advisor, couldn't see what I saw for the future of science and all that I thought I had to offer the science community and the world for that matter. My physical abilities weren't an issue in my eyes. I could do just about anything anyone else could do when it came to running, jumping, exercising, bike riding, and practically anything you could think of—I could do it. They misunderstood me and my zeal for the pursuit of my vision for my life. However, their discouragement just caused me to study that much harder. I applied to college and was accepted at the University of Georgia. I double majored in biology and biochemistry with a minor in computer programming since the school had an excellent computer department. I advanced to the top of my class in most of the sciences and also in the creative arts. With surprise, my college advisors also rejected my career plans as well as my vision for the dental profession. At first, their rejection was disappointing, but after a few days, I just turned up the heat with my research and study and applied myself even further. I created all kinds of proposals for biotechnological ideas and concepts.

One idea that changed my life as well as the life of many others was what I called the "Big Idea." One Friday, I was returning from a dental visit shortly after having a dental filling placed in my molar tooth on the right side of my jaw. My jaw was still numb from the anesthesia. I looked down at the GPS system on the console of the car, as I chewed my gum and popped a blow bubble. It was at that moment I thought, *Why not have a microchip placed in the filling of the tooth? This way the chip could locate any missing person or even calculate data like body temperature or even create waves of frequency to combat dental disease.* This idea would have to be researched and tested. And so I did: every weekend I would squeeze my way to the professors at the university and gain every thought they had, especially the engineers. In the midst of my college education and pursuit for the development of my new idea, I applied at the Medical College of Georgia in Augusta and was invited for an interview at the school. By this time, I had three years of college under my belt.

I thought the interview at the dental school went well; however, I didn't get accepted that year because so many students had already been chosen from a nearby dental university that had just closed down that year due to the economic crisis and soaring educational costs. Disappointed, but with resolve, I told the dental committee that I would be back the next year to reapply.

While waiting to apply for the next year, I wanted to make use of my time so I found a job working in a biochemical lab at the University of Georgia. My job was simple in that I mainly assisted the other PhD chemists who were on the research team. My responsibilities were small, but I thought the job description would look good on my résumé for dental school. Shortly afterwards, I reapplied to dental school and received my acceptance letter in December, a wonderful Christmas gift.

My acceptance at the Medical College of Georgia renewed my faith that dreams do come true. Against all odds, I knew then that I was on my way to develop my vision and accomplish my goals: to be a dentist, to change the world, and to make it a better place. I pushed the envelope and worked very hard while in dental school and continued my research on the idea of the GPS microchip dental system (the Big Idea). After graduating from dental school, I continued my professional education and did an extra year in hospital dentistry at Talmage Hospital in Augusta, where I practiced advanced anesthesia and implant training and became quite efficient in the field of dental implants.

~ 3 ~

The Development of the Mikecrodent Chip

After I studied and learned as much as I could about the technical hardware of devices similar to the one I wanted for my dental-filling microchip project, I called and asked Dr. Samuel Lee, a senior professor in the computer design department at the University of Georgia, about my desire for a specifically designed microchip. Dr. Lee was intrigued by the idea and referred me to a company in Fresno, California, that made small chips that handled the type of data I was looking for. I didn't know if such a device existed small enough to implant on a human tooth. If anyone in the field had the capability of manufacturing the chip, it would be this company. Dr. Lee told me that the company's name was Microfix. He took me back into his office and pulled up the contact name, Steven Hill, from his Rolodex. I thanked Dr. Lee and he wished me luck and success and told me to stay in touch with him.

The next Wednesday I called Steven and told him that I was looking for a microchip and gave him the dimensions that I needed. Steven told me that he thought he might have the chip, but that I would have to come out there and meet with him to evaluate the thickness and power of the chip to see if it was what I was looking for. We scheduled an appointment for the next Friday at 12:30 p.m. I caught a plane out to California and met with Steven. We had a productive conversation as I examined the chip. Steven's company had developed similar types of microchips two years earlier, one of which was used as a subdermal chip designed for implantation under the skin of the forearm.

This system was referred to as a RFID (radio frequency identification) system. Basic components consisted of a small antenna, a transceiver with a decoder, and a transponder called a tag. The software allowed all of the components to function together. These tags or transponders could be electronically programmed with different kinds of data. Both large and small data bits could be handled with this device and were encryption capable. The antenna, when combined with a decoder, was used as a RFID reader. The reader would pick up and decode the signal from the transponder or tag, and the data would then be transferred to a corporate database where it was recorded, stored, and analyzed for alternate uses.

There were, at that time, two main types of RFID technologies: active and passive. The active RFID system was the one that I wanted to explore in depth. The device contained a battery capable of transmitting radio signals on its own. The passive device, on the other hand, required an external supply to transmit signals. Both devices contained an integrated circuit with the potential for integration in an infinite number of applications. These devices were currently being used for many different activities and included radio activator switches. The RFID tags, along with their radio activator switches, were already in wide use in the United States by that time for use in credit card microchip identification, library book identification, retail store items for purchase, prison inmate tracking devices, animal identification, passports identification, and too many other applications to mention. If RFID tags and concomitant technology could be applied to an implantable chip safely and small enough for implantation on a child's tooth, my plan would be realized.

After searching through the patents and records of experimental dentistry, I found not one scientist or practitioner working toward the development of an implantable device for children's identification using a microchip. The devices had been successfully used for protecting children in some select schools, but the microchips were placed on the children's clothing and were not attached to the child's body. This feature made it too easy for criminals to remove and inactivate the device, making it useless to me.

Steven told me that these devices were controversial. Many parents questioned the safety of the device. Then, there were the privacy laws with public outcry over a system of this type and its possible misuse, although in my mind I could not fathom how the recovery of a kidnapped child could compromise a person's privacy. I thanked Steven for his concerns, but I assured him that I would move forward immediately to acquire the chip technology and prioritize its manufacture.

There were also concerns of hacking the devices to steal data from the chip's database and identification information, especially the ones that were not encrypted. The chip also had its susceptibility to computer viruses.

The microchip that was being used as a human implant for identification purposes with data capability did exist, and it was FDA approved, but it likewise was too large to be used in dentistry because it was about an inch long. This system was a subdermal chip placed directly under the skin of the forearm. The subdermal human implant microchip was used to activate switches to open specific doors and locks. I was interested in this chip. One of the drawbacks that concerned me was that the RFID required an antenna. Also, it needed a small battery that required recharging at intervals. I did want the high signal power offered by this model, but the length size of the antenna that was required with it was too large for use in the mouth. I told Steven my concern, and he told me that he would take my specifications' requests to the committee board and see what they had to offer. I left and went back home. I spent hours studying the RFID system and read every book I could get my hands on that involved the subject.

I also looked at other companies, but they really didn't compare to Steven's technological advancements and small size to high power ratio microchips.

Another concern for me was the battery life for the device. Steven told me that a Russian company had recently developed a battery that could last for several years, depending on the power drain that pulled from the device. Unfortunately, the battery's size was too large for my needs. I went back to the university and met with Professor Lee and two computer engineers to present my findings. They were helpful in advising me on what I should do. They told me that I needed to find a company with the technology capable of designing such a chip first and then find another company that would work with me to design a battery that would furnish adequate power.

The battery power requirements for the chip I wanted would only need a very small energy source since my device would be using a GPS chip that would be used during emergency activation only.

Their advice seemed reasonable since I first had to have the chip in order to enter into experimental trials of battery development. However, I went home overwhelmed by the complexity of the whole matter.

I was certain that 21st-century technology was advancing exponentially and would come through for me if I could convince the companies that my vision for the protection of innocent children was both profitable and valuable in this world. My thinking was that if you could "think it," then you could "make it." I continued the pursuit for the device that I wanted for several months, but to no avail. Then four months later, I got a call from Steven. He told me that they were looking at a new chip that was in its early stages of development from one of their mother companies. Steven told me that he thought it was the chip that I was looking for. I got excited and flew back up to California for a meeting with him at his company headquarters. I agreed with Steven that it had most of the features that I was seeking. I wanted the microchip. It was close to the size and power that I wanted, and the antenna was built into the device. This was very exciting to me.

The problem was the price tag. When I discovered that the chip was $5,500, I was shocked. When Steven saw my dismay, he eased my fear somewhat by telling me that an order of 1,000 chips would bring the price down to $1,500. After they started mass-producing them, the price would continue to drop, as was the usual market trend in the computer world. I thought for a moment and said, "Okay, I want to get one now. I will use it as a test model on myself and see if it is what I am looking for." Although it would cost nearly two million dollars to purchase 1,000 devices, I knew that I could pull this off, especially if my prototype performed as I expected. I knew that there was a market for the chip. With high demand, the price would drop even more. I believed in my vision for this device and felt it was capable of starting an exciting new development in the field of science and health, and I would be the first to explore the dental aspect of it, from its infancy stages.

The following year, the chip was available for sale on the market, and I immediately purchased one. I received my first microchip in December near Christmas. What a Christmas gift it was! I now had something to work with and a company that could mass-produce the device, provided it functioned to my satisfaction. As soon as I got the device, I wrote a patent for the specialized use of the microchip in the field of dentistry. The patent described the device, its purpose, handling, placement, and use, in what I termed "microchip dentistry." I named the device the "Mikecrodent" chip. I got the name from the Biblical archangel "Michael" and used the short version of Mike. The small "c" was for Carla and the small "r" was the first letter in my name. I called a patent attorney. After another $5,000, I had a patent for microchip's usage in the dental field, more specifically for my idea of GPS usage with dental applications.

I felt that this was just the start of a most magnificent journey in the field of microchip dentistry. I was certain that it would open up a completely new area for dentistry and would offer options that were not available until my device was invented. Although it would take years to perfect the device and even additional years to get FDA approval, I was excited and felt I was onto a brand-new era in my field.

I then called Steven, and we programmed the device for GPS settings and started activating the system within a few weeks. Now that I had my device GPS-ready, I had to find a satellite service that would receive signals that the chip emitted. I called Professor Lee at the university who told me that there was a Japanese company that had leased their satellite to some of the GPS developers. He suggested that I call immediately. I was given permission to access their satellite for one year for $1,500. I signed the contract and obtained code ordinances for frequency collaboration. The Mikecrodent chip came with its own serial number and code for communicating with the satellite signal. This code synchronized the frequency, which connected the communications from the device to the satellite and then back to a software-locating tool. The software was commonly sold in computer stores for about one-hundred dollars.

Now I had my system up and running. I would just sit back and watch the satellite track the device as I went from place to place. I developed a method for attaching the device to my tooth. First, I did a mock trial by taking a fake microchip, i.e. a small microchip from a credit card, cutting it to size and attaching it to an extracted tooth. This enabled me to visualize how I wanted to place the actual device in the mouth. After I perfected the technique using the extracted teeth, I placed a Mikecrodent chip in one of my own dental restorations on my upper-right molar tooth, and tracked myself online via the satellite GPS system.

My chip was sophisticated. I continued my work with Steven at Microfix to upgrade them, modify them, and integrate new and multifunctional capabilities. I worked with them to perform a variety of functions.

Developing a chip with such small dimensions was one of the most difficult aspects to pursue in the early stages of the Mikecrodent-chip project. There were other GPS systems breaking onto the market, but the smallest one that had any reasonable signal strength was about one inch by one inch, which was much too large to use in the mouth. There was one chip that suddenly came out on the market about the size of a grain of rice, but the signal strength was so low that it wouldn't even pick up on the satellite in many of the major cities like New York, Cincinnati, Atlanta, Dallas, and Washington, D.C. The device that I was developing possessed adequate signal strength, capable of tracking an abducted child taken into the inner city amid the conflict of multiple signaling devices. The signal would quickly and accurately accomplish the task, thereby reducing the likelihood that the child would be lost. The chip was to be small enough that it could be handled with the fingers, but not readily visible or obvious to the common layperson's eye. After another year of development, while working with Microfix, I was able to get my wish. My chip was now two millimeters by two millimeters by one-half millimeter and was the smallest and most powerful chip available of its kind.

I immediately placed the device on the market for dentists to purchase. The Mikecrodent kit was about $1,200 for a simple GPS-tracking system. The kit included one chip with its distinctive serial number, the software system, a DVD instructional guide, and one year of free system support. The kit also included a fifty-percent-off coupon that could be used for the required introductory course. There were several courses available for a fee. These were useful for the dentist who wanted to learn more about additional features of the system. The chip became even more costly if the company added additional software. Since the device could now even have a motherboard installed, features could readily be added. The motherboard was the platform that the chip used for additional features, similar to a motherboard in a home computer. Plug-in devices, such as a video card and 3D capabilities, could monitor vital signs from a patient while a sound card could reproduce sounds. My chip was quite different in its variability of use. After the technology had been achieved, I began mass production to lower the cost so that practically everyone could benefit from its protection and use.

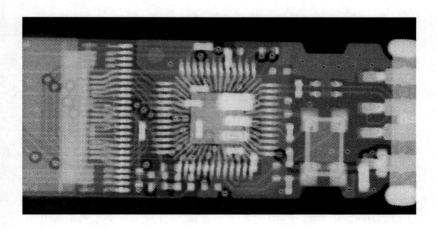

I eventually reduced the cost to $850. Many insurance companies would pay for the system. Other insurance companies offered discounts on the policy owner's premium. Some of the insurance companies began to recognize the benefit of Mikecrodent's medical potential.

I knew that these chips could be placed in children's teeth for identity purposes, as well as for tracking them in the event of an abduction. I thought about Carla and how my life would have been different if Carla had one of these chips placed in her tooth as a child. I was sure that it would have saved her life. The small size of the chip was comfortable for patients to have in the mouth and nondetectible to the untrained eye of the criminal. The original GPS-tracking systems that were used had to be large and attached to the child's clothing. Because of the size and the criminal's knowledge of the device, the criminal would immediately see the device and just remove it, thereby deactivating it. A nonprofessional didn't have the trained eye to detect the Mikecrodent chip in the mouth. As far as the criminal knew, the chip could be on any tooth in the mouth and could be in a filling or bonded with white composite resin, camouflaging it to the amateur eye. It required a dentist who was trained in one of my Mikecrodent courses to detect and remove a chip in the mouth. It would soon become law that no one could remove a Mikecrodent chip without a written release and a permit provided by the court. Obtaining a permit to remove a Mikecrodent chip from a child's tooth was difficult and time-consuming, because the courts understood the importance and usefulness of the device. These qualities served as a deterrent to criminals who now hated me so much that my life was in danger.

One Friday night, I was eating at a restaurant when I got a phone call that someone had just backed into my car outside. While I was outside inspecting my car, several shots were fired at me. I hit the pavement for safety and called

911. The shooters must have thought I went down, thinking I had been shot. Fortunately, that was not the case. I hit the pavement purely out of fear and natural instinct. This episode convinced me that I definitely had serious enemies. I was convinced that it was an activist who opposed the use of the Mikecrodent chip.

Shortly after this experience, I was contacted by the CIA for an interview. The CIA was interested in my patent and the potential it had for the agency. They were already secretly using a similar system and had their own satellite in place. The director of the CIA was interested in my concept and use of the chip in child abductions and its dental applications for their own department. They were considering using the chip in their agents' teeth for their protection and location. Other devices were easily detected and visible, making them useless. The organization became increasingly interested in my device. They knew that my chip had potential and that I was the most experienced in this field of technology. They also wanted to consider it for military use, for soldiers in combat and fighter pilots that were shot down and captured. Military rescue operations would benefit greatly from this technology. The discussions that the Agency and I had were very top secret. I had to sign a written hush contract, committing to my silence of the conversations and ideas of the Agency. My code of silence was an honor for me, as I had great respect for the Agency.

The chip was usually bonded to an upper molar on the cheek side of a tooth with the integrated circuit exposed to the mouth. The buccal surface or cheek side of the molar was a nonchewing surface that would minimize the bite forces and chewing pressures that commonly occurred in the oral cavity. However, I still advised users to avoid hard, sticky candies and ice because the device could break or bend or even dislodge from the tooth. This juxtaposition created an open circuit in the oral cavity, enabling the device to perform several body analyses. While in contact with saliva, the device could detect antibody concentration, which could provide many immunological implications.

There were many other uses for the Mikecrodent chip. The chip could also be modified for alcoholics to wear for help in managing their disease. The device could be equipped with the chemical analysis software and detect breath alcohol concentrations and would record data that would detect alcohol and even drug use and would prove especially helpful in monitoring recovering alcohol and drug users as well as DUI offenders.

The chip could be used to detect tooth grinding or night bruxism. It could be used for the elderly who were debilitated, alerting caretakers of the person's location and medical status. This would be especially helpful in home-assisted care patients when a nurse was available for only a few hours a day, as well as for remaining hours where a health-care professional was not available. The device would be invaluable in keeping tabs on these patients.

Using the device in the prison system would readily guarantee that an escapee would be recaptured possibly before having a chance to injure or kill the guards or someone after they escaped. The chip could also create a painful episode of pulse waves to control a prisoner's behavior, rather than riotous collisions with prison guards and endangering them as well. The tooth pain mode might seem like aggressive torture, but the intensity could be controlled with each inmate. It was considered by many to be a more humane and natural form of discipline than straitjackets, mace, Taser guns, and brutal force.

The chip could detect body pH and blood-oxygen levels through pulse oximetry and detect heart rate. It also could measure respiration during inhalation and expiration and barometric pressure, once baseline measurements were calculated and compared. This data could be determined and then be very useful, especially to the military. In theory, if a soldier in combat were injured on the battleground, the device would determine and measure vital signs and relay the data to the satellite, so that the medical doctors, back at the base, could better diagnose and advise the appropriate mode of response for the medic to treat an injured soldier. The soldier could be located by helicopter transport since the device had the global positional tracking system feature.

I was also working with voice recognition where small key vibrations from the vocal cords could send a message to the satellite. For example, password phrases like "combat 911" would emit a message relay that indicated an emergency signal while in combat. The alert message would then be assessed by military officials to gather intelligence. The system could relay back to the soldier a pulse in Morse code to communicate messages. These small pulses were not painful and would feel like a tingling sensation on the tooth. The sensation would be somewhat like touching a weak 9-volt battery to the tongue, but with a much lighter stimulation. Even this tingling sensation could be calibrated for the comfort levels of the individual soldier. This feature could provide several advantages to the soldier. For example, if the soldier were in a place where the radio couldn't be used, in quiet and silent code combat moments, the satellite could alert the soldier of an approaching enemy. I was also working on music radio waves radiating from the device. It has been said that people have heard radio music in their dental fillings. Dental silver fillings have been known to do this. If a person were in the right place at the right time with the right position of radio waves, the silver fillings could act as a small transistor and focus the radio wave into sound. Whether this theory is true or not, I began to add music and sound to the chip to see its implications, especially for the hearing impaired. As mentioned earlier, the chip could act as a motherboard computer and interact with a computer for data calculations and data storage.

I met with the three CEOs of some of the world's largest software companies to discuss the Mikecrodent technology. The discussion was fruitful and promising. They also talked about the possibilities of the chip being placed in other parts of the body, like the feet, to be cemented to the toenail, implanted in the ear, placed on the fingernail, under the scalp, or under the eyelid. The eyelid design had a small laser projector that projected an image onto the eyelid while the eye was closed. This system used the eyelid as a projector screen. It was minimally invasive with very few risks. One of the most prominent CEOs wanted to schedule a meeting with professionals in several disciplines to brainstorm other uses for his Mikecrodent chip. He wanted an ophthalmologist on board as a professional advisor. I had quite a business with my system and by this time had a great deal of money invested in it. I hoped to begin paying off my debts with the profit from the Mikecrodent chip company.

One year into the company's growth, a breakthrough came with a "home run." A little girl named Casie Stakks had been kidnapped. She was wearing the Mikecrodent device. Police were able to locate her within fifteen hours of her abduction.

When news of the capture of Casie's abductor hit the media and it was announced she was found unharmed, orders poured into company headquarters. The kidnapper was Tom Penn from Tennessee. Tom was a 58-year-old troubled man who was a drug user with a rap sheet five pages long. As the investigation intensified, more evidence surfaced to indicate this man might have been involved in other kidnappings. They found little Casie in Tom Penn's apartment basement and further evidence to indicate he was preparing to abuse her. The basement was thoroughly searched for evidence. All the evidence they needed to convict and sentence him was there, in addition to evidence that other children had been held captive in this dark, horrible torture pit. The Mikecrodent chip probably saved Casie's life and the lives of others who would have been abducted by this monster.

The quick capture of Penn sent a loud message to other potential offenders. Mikecrodent Company flourished as its value was substantiated; its credibility and usefulness were proven in the real world. Once media coverage went worldwide, orders poured into Mikecrodent daily, more than it could deliver. Mikecrodent was mass-producing the chip around the clock with three shifts producing as fast as possible. As global demands for the device skyrocketed, so did the demand for trained dentists who could implant the chip. I required all dentists to first take the introductory Mikecrodent course if they intended to purchase and implant the Mikecrodent device. I taught the course with a team of experts. My schedule was hectic as I traveled around the world. The team included an FBI agent, a policeman, an attorney, a computer technician, a hygienist, and a physician. The police official explained their involvement with the dentist and how the GPS device would enable them to track the children quickly and with accuracy. The computer technician taught the participants how to use the software that was packaged with the device. Each dentist had to know how to place the device properly and how to synchronize the chip, so that it could be activated.

The course taught dentists how to enter the required initial entry data for the patient, such as the child's name, Social Security number, home address, race, age, height, hair color, body weight, eye color, digital scan of their fingerprints, dental radiographs, facial photographs, emergency phone numbers for contact, and any health information that was a medical alert, including allergies and any medications they were taking. All of this data had to be logged in to the computer before the satellite could properly read and lock a signal for each person wearing the dental microchip. Once a signal was achieved and locked on the user, then the device was in sleep mode until it was activated as needed.

The attorney addressed the legal ramifications of the device, such as the liability of the dentist and the risk involved. If, for example, the device were placed and not functional when called upon in an emergency, the dentist had to prove that the proper protocols had been followed and documented at a "standard of care" level. The standard of care protocols required dentists to properly evaluate the monitoring device at yearly dental recall exams and follow through with confirmation of the required calibration measurements. When health-care professionals deal in children's lives, even the smallest error could not be tolerated.

The hygienist was on the team to teach dentists how to properly clean the teeth without damaging the device. A special dental tool was used to clean around the tooth that held the device. The use of conventional dental instruments could harm its sensitive circuitry and alter its effectiveness.

The medical doctor on the team instructed the dentists about the medical aspects and use of the device. New medical applications for the Mikecrodent chips were being developed in the research and design department at my company. Several medical applications would be hitting the market within six months. The dentists needed to know how, what, when, and where the device was to be used.

For example, for older patients, specific functions like the pulse oximetry feature were useful in measuring and recording blood-oxygen levels in medically compromised people. This model was somewhat more complicated where the doctor had to understand blood-analysis interpretation.

However, for children who only had the GPS locator system model 1100, the doctor simply followed the guideline tutorial, which was formatted in the software program. The program guide instructed the doctor to type in the child's medical information to be inserted into the database. All dentists were required to know the capabilities of the devices, even for those they would never be monitoring themselves.

I taught dentists how to properly place and remove the device and elaborated on the medical and dental applications of the chip. For example, the 2200 model had the capability of treating tooth pain, dental decay, and periodontal disease. The scientific data behind these treatments had to comply with the concept of "Evidence-based Dentistry," an approach in medicine that was defined by the medical community as "the integration of the best evidence with clinical expertise and patient values." The American Dental Association refined the concept for dentistry and defined Evidence-based Dentistry as "an approach to oral health care that requires the judicious integration of systematic assessments of clinically relevant scientific evidence, relating to the patient's oral and medical condition and history together with the dentist's clinical expertise and the patient's treatment needs and preferences." I had done my homework over the past ten years on the project and knew what the device could do and what its limitations were. My primary reason for so much hands-on involvement was to teach dentists the "technique sensitive" procedures that were required when inserting the device in order to minimize operator error. For the chip to function properly when called upon in an emergency situation, the implantation technique had to be flawless.

~ 4 ~

The BBB Interference

Not everyone was thrilled or impressed by the Mikecrodent system, especially a group of activists called the BBB, Big Bad Brother. The group originated from the Big Brother era when privacy laws were being challenged. The group thought that my device was a direct violation of an individual's privacy rights, just another ploy in a long list of attempts to usurp the freedoms we should be guaranteed by the Constitution. I, along with my attorneys, would meet with the BBB annually in an attempt to forge a common ground with them. They refused to acknowledge the value of the tracking mechanism. Their rhetoric was unfortunately supported by a large group of antigovernment extremists. To the BBB, it was all an invasion of privacy, and that was their conclusion at every meeting, even when I mentioned the statistics of child abduction and what the chip could do to help missing children.

On one occasion, I brought two mothers to a meeting. Both mothers praised my efforts for being active and aggressive in dealing with child abduction because each had lost a child to kidnappers. Not one of the group members showed any compassion for these heartbroken women. One of the mothers attempted to reason with them, but her pleas went unanswered. When they heard about the chip, both took their other children to the dentist to have the chip implanted. She said that, until then, no one had actively done anything to apprehend the kidnappers. She said, "What does a mother do in this type of situation?" With many tears, she said, "I won't let this happen to my children again. Ray is doing something about it. We support Ray's technology. We have the right to protect our children. Criminals only have to worry about losing their rights if they commit a crime and wind up in jail. If that happens and criminals go to jail, then they have made the decision to lose their right to privacy."

The men argued vehemently, "We know what's happening with this chip technology. Maybe, in the beginning, it was innocent, but now it's being used to track everyone the Government thinks is suspicious. The Government can track our health data and use the data to deny us health insurance. You are the ones who haven't thought about the ramifications of this technology. It's the same as being marked by the Beast."

Communication broke down when a heated discussion ensued. These men would not even agree to the chip's application as a means of locating missing children. They kept pushing the legal system to take action on their part to stop the device from being used.

I told the BBB many times, "You do what you have to do, and I will do what I have to do." We respected the activists' right to disagree with our point of view and their rejection of the use of Mikecrodent. I was passionate about the chip. I never told them the real reason why I had developed the chip, the kidnapping of my little sister. Our motivation was pure. I wanted the group to stop trying to influence lawmakers to discontinue the use of Mikecrodent. I thought that individuals should have the right to use the device to prevent what happened to Carla.

It seemed to me that only criminals would be the ones to reject its use. Why in the world would anyone want to interfere with a protection device for parents who wanted extra protection for their children? Another crucial point that we made to the critics of the Mikecrodent system was that the chip was only activated in an emergency situation when a child was abducted. The chip could remain in sleep mode for years until it was activated. There was no tracking of children in any way except for an emergency, when a child's life was at stake.

At the time when this controversy was taking place, there was a demand for the device. Several children who had disappeared were found dead after they had been kidnapped. That seemed to be the trend. The kidnappers didn't just take the children and abuse them, as horrific as that was. They would most often kill the children after they abused them. This common occurrence demanded strong attention and action, and I felt I was the one to help combat the problem.

~ 5 ~
Ray's Faith

My faith in Jesus, The Christ, began at age twelve and grew to the point where I later became involved in world missions and treated patients around the world with implant and anesthesia techniques. The mission travels included Peru, Russia, Cuba, India, China, Vietnam, Africa, Bolivia, and Brazil. I eventually grew towards the revelation that God loved me more than I could realize every single day and in every way. God's sacrifice of His one and only Son for me demonstrated the full measure of His love. I wanted to share that unconditional love with as many people as I could. I read the Scriptures daily and enjoyed learning about the personality of my Jesus.

I started going to a church in my area that was quite different from the others in the community. I went to this church because it was nondenominational and closely followed the New Testament Scriptures in an apostolic structure. In the book of Acts, there were apostles, prophets, teachers, evangelists, and pastors, each having a gift for specific use in the church. This church had many of the spiritual gifts and exercised them with power, including the prophetic gifting. When I began attending there, I didn't know what a prophet was or if prophecy even existed. Little did I know that I would soon discover what prophecy meant in a direct and personal way.

One month after I first began attending the church, one of the prophets prophesied to me. He walked up to me face to face during the service, as I stood in the congregation, and laid his hand upon my head and began to speak to me. At first, it seemed odd and embarrassing but I managed to keep my composure. He knew of my name from friends, but I didn't know him. I was somewhat excited and didn't know what to expect. He said that he believed that God had given him a word to impart to me and then said, "Just as David in the Bible took down the mighty giant, Goliath, with a small stone, so will you, Ray, take down a mighty evil giant, and you will spiritually stand out for and advance the Kingdom of God to show the mighty power of His marvelous works."

When I first heard the prophecy spoken over me, I really didn't understand the significance of a true prophet of God, nor did I perceive the magnitude of this truth being spoken over me. I had never experienced anything like that before. I didn't know what to do or say. I just kept my head bowed while standing and smiled and said, "Thank you, LORD." That night I went straight home and found the Scriptures that talked about King David in 1st Samuel, chapter 17, and found these words:

> *Now the Philistines gathered their armies for battle; they were gathered at Socoh, which belongs to Judah, and encamped between Socoh and Azekah, in Ephes-dammim. Saul and the Israelites gathered and encamped in the valley of Elah, and formed ranks against the Philistines. The Philistines stood on the mountain on the one side, and Israel stood on the mountain on the other side, with a valley between them.*
>
> *And there came out from the camp of the Philistines a champion named Goliath, of Gath, whose height was six cubits and a span (almost 10 feet). He had a helmet of bronze on his head, and he was armed with a coat of mail; the weight of the coat was five thousand shekels of bronze. He had greaves of bronze on his legs and a javelin of bronze slung between his shoulders. The shaft of his spear was like a weaver's beam, and his spear's head weighed six hundred shekels of iron; and his shield-bearer went before him.*

He stood and shouted to the ranks of Israel, "Why have you come out to draw up for battle? Am I not a Philistine, and are you not servants of Saul? Choose a man for yourselves, and let him come down to me. If he is able to fight with me and kill me, then we will be your servants; but if I prevail against him and kill him, then you shall be our servants and serve us." And the Philistine said, "Today I defy the ranks of Israel! Give me a man, that we may fight together."

When Saul and all Israel heard these words of the Philistine, they were dismayed and greatly afraid.

David said, "The LORD who delivered me out of the paw of the lion and out of the paw of the bear, He will deliver me out of the hand of this Philistine." And Saul said to David, "Go, and the LORD be with you."

Then he took his staff in his hand and chose five smooth stones out of the brook and put them in his shepherd's bag, in his pouch, and his sling was in his hand, and he drew near the Philistine.

The Philistine came on and drew near to David, with his shield-bearer in front of him. When the Philistine looked and saw David, he disdained him, for he was only a youth, ruddy and handsome in appearance. The Philistine said to David, "Am I a dog, that you come to me with sticks?" And the Philistine cursed David by his gods. The Philistine said to David, "Come to me, and I will give your flesh to the birds of the air and to the wild animals of the field."

But David said to the Philistine, "You come to me with sword and spear and javelin; but I come to you in the name of the LORD of hosts, the God of the armies of Israel, whom you have defied. This very day the LORD will deliver you into my hand, and I will strike you down and cut off your head; and I will give the dead bodies of the Philistine army this very day to the birds of the air and to the wild animals of the earth, so that all the earth may know that there is a God in Israel, and that all this assembly may know the LORD saves not with sword and spear; for the battle is the LORD'S, and He will give you into our hands."

When the Philistine came forward to meet David, David ran quickly toward the battle line to meet the Philistine.

David put his hand into his bag and took out a stone and slung it, and it struck the Philistine, sinking into his forehead, and he fell on his face to the earth. So David prevailed over the Philistine with a sling and with a stone, and struck down the Philistine and slew him. But no sword was in David's hand. So he ran and stood over the Philistine, took his sword and drew it out of its sheath, and killed him, and cut off his head with it. When the Philistines saw that their mighty champion was dead, they fled.

I read this Scripture at least once a week for months and would envision myself in David's sandals. I meditated daily in an attempt to understand why this was spoken to me at this point in my life. As the next several days passed, the Scripture passage of David and the Giant remained deep within my spirit and heart, but with many pieces of the puzzle missing at this point. The words spoken over me in the prophecy repeated themselves over and over, every day, mostly everywhere I went. I couldn't shake the words from my heart, nor was I able to grasp the meaning of the prophetic message. Afterwards, I kept the prophetic message in the back of my mind, but continued on to read the Bible.

The church was actively involved in the ministry of world missions and supported my commitment to missions. The church had presbytery that helped to disciple and equip the church leaders for ministry outside the church walls. I enjoyed traveling around the world and helping people through the dental and medical clinics. The clinics were a platform that helped show people that God loved them, and that He wanted to help them. I had the privilege of seeing many different cultures with various beliefs. This didn't bother me nor did it intimidate me. I just embraced the opportunity to connect with the people and usually overpowered the area with tender loving care. The atmosphere of love that was created during the mission clinics allowed the mission team to improve the lives of those we touched and gave, myself especially, favor from the community leaders. I often had the key to the city or area where we would locate the mission setup. I often had the freedom to do what I wanted within reason and go just about anywhere I wished in the foreign land, as long as I took one of the local chaperones with me who had political privileges.

One early April Friday morning, I received a phone call from my best friend of twenty years, Lee Castillo. Lee, a self-made multimillionaire, lived in the mountains of North Carolina. He would call me every year to go trout fishing on one of his mountain streams. He owned property in the mountains that had some of the state's best trout streams running through the land. Since the land was privately owned, there were few people fishing the streams. If someone did have the privilege to fish one of Lee's streams, it was expensive, approximately $500 per hour. Lee seldom allowed people to fish on his property, unless he knew them personally. Lee and I worked on our schedules and planned to go fishing the following weekend. The next weekend I packed my fishing supplies and met Lee at his house. As we were driving down to the river, we began talking about some of the most memorable moments that had taken place in our lives over the last ten years. Lee asked me, "What comes to mind when you think about your incredible moments?"

I said, "There have been many." I pondered for a moment and then said, "I remember once, when I was in Peru on a mission trip, we were on a small medical missions' boat on the Amazon River. We would stop at various villages and provide medical and dental treatment to the people. One afternoon, after clinic we gave out toys and dolls to the children in a small village. I remember the look on one child's face when I gave her the doll. Her little, dirty face gleamed with amazement. She just kept her eyes fixed on the doll as she wandered off into the jungle carefully holding the doll in front of her as if it were a real baby. I watched her for several minutes as she walked into the jungle out of my sight.

"After we treated the people in the villages, we would give them a Gideons Bible in their own language and share the Gospel with them. We told them to find a local village church and to read their Bibles every day.

"Another event that was memorable to me happened in Venezuela. When I was passing out Bibles, we ran out. We would usually take a box of fifty small Bibles with us and distribute them after the clinic had closed for the evening. The children would be instructed to form a single line, and with one child at a time coming forth to receive their Bible, I would hand it over to them. The problem was that there were more than fifty children that day wanting Bibles in their own language, and some of the children saw that I didn't have enough for everyone. Once the children realized that some of the children at the back of the line might not get a Bible, they began to panic and grab the Bibles with great force. At one point, one of the children pulled the Bible from my hands with all the strength he had. I handed the last one to a little boy. The next child behind him knew there wasn't enough to go around and that he wasn't going to get one. The look of disappointment on his face changed me for life. I vowed that I would do everything I could to send Bibles around the world."

~ 6 ~

Ray's Family

Two years into private practice, I met my wife, Trudy. We married in December. Trudy was a "knockout." She was a beautiful woman about five feet and five inches tall with thick long dark-black shiny hair and big crystal-clear blue eyes. I just loved Trudy's small-framed curvy little body. Trudy was fast on her feet and took very good care of herself. She watched everything she ate to ensure it was healthy, nutritious, and low fat. She was always determining the fat grams and carbohydrates of her food before she ate. She exercised every day, and it was all I could do to keep up with her. I also worked out and exercised, but not to the extent that Trudy did. I was thin in stature but with good body tone and form. I took multivitamins, mineral supplements, and antioxidant supplements. Trudy also took vitamin and mineral supplements and antioxidants. She wore sunscreen when she went outside to protect her beautiful skin. Trudy was a big fan of *I Love Lucy*. She collected everything she could that had Lucy's name on it.

Trudy also had a little dog that was the highlight of her day. Reece was a poodle and Chihuahua mix with long brown hair. She was afraid of the dark and loved to sit by the heater in the winter months.

Trudy was an intelligent lady with manners and grace. She lived by principles and always did the right thing, even if it was difficult. She had strong faith in God and was well versed in the Scriptures. She also had a strong personality: self-assured and confident. She liked to do things her way and usually was right. I didn't have a problem with her strength and confidence. I admired her and appreciated her ability to make tough decisions on the spot in an efficient manner. Trudy helped me in mostly everything I would undertake. Often, my shoulders and neck would bother me with muscle spasms from the posture that I held while treating patients. Trudy would give me a rubdown. She was great at giving massages. I looked forward to this time together. It wasn't long before I knew Trudy was the woman that I had been looking for all of my life. For our first wedding anniversary, Trudy got me what I had been wanting for a long time. It was a golden necklace of the Star of David. I wore it everywhere I went, never removing it.

Once, I had to have a neck x-ray for the chiropractor to evaluate my spine. I refused to remove the necklace so the x-ray could be taken. I finally gave in and briefly removed the necklace for the radiologist, but immediately replaced it. I really liked my Star of David necklace. Trudy was in tune with the desires of my heart. I often would say, "This woman knows what she is doing and knows how to get things done."

Trudy had two adult children and five grandchildren. Trudy and I had custody of three of the five grandchildren. Christopher, Nicole, and Mikaella lived with us, and Brittany and Kyle lived next door with their parents. Christopher, eleven years old, was a bright, blue-eyed charmer and very helpful around the house. He was the only little boy in the family, and I enjoyed having another male to do our mechanical tasks with. Christopher was a fast learner and liked to know about everything. If you were on the computer, then he wanted to know what you were doing, and he wanted to know how to do it himself. He especially wanted to learn at bedtime. He knew this might buy him some extra time to stay up later at night. Being aware that he was reluctant to get his needed sleep, I made sure Christopher was in bed by 9:30 p.m. on weeknights and

11:00 p.m. on weekends. We played games together. Christopher nearly always won. He liked it that way. His confidence was inspiring, especially for those who met him for the first time. One time I told Christopher that he was very smart. Christopher said, "Yes, Papa Ray, I know," with a big smile on his face. He excelled at playing the guitar and would play and sing as he created his own songs, just as I did when I was a young boy. Formatroners (small transformer toys) were his favorite toys. His collection covered every wall in his room. He would often stand in front of the mirror, changing his clothes two to three times a day, just so he could look neat and presentable. I loved to see Christopher gleam with assurance.

Then there was Nicole, thirteen years old, and very talented. She was highly organized and loved to flip and show off. She was a girly person who took gymnastics and would often show her flips at home for Trudy and me. She performed gymnastics for the family every Friday night. Nicole was gifted in administration and focused on speech and communication as she played with the other children. She would help them learn different skills in every sport. She often would ask deep, penetrating questions. Many of which I had no answer: questions like "Why can life be so difficult and hard sometimes?" "Why did God ask Adam where he was, right after he sinned in the Garden of Eden?" She said she knew that God knew where Adam was so, "Why did He ask him this question?" It was interesting to hear what Nicole had to say when she was in her thinking mode. I thought she was very intelligent for her age and so did she.

Mikaella was fifteen and also very beautiful. All the boys loved to talk to her, and she liked talking to the boys. She was personable and softhearted. Mikaella liked to ponder a lot. She often worried about her parents as well as Trudy and me. Mikaella was at the age where she wasn't really sure what she wanted. For example, once, she had a birthday breakfast and contemplated inviting her friend Brianna. She kept saying she wasn't sure if she should invite her friend or not. Trudy asked her what she felt like she wanted to do. She would say her famous line…"I don't know, I guess so." But she was okay with this phase in her life. It didn't bother her that she couldn't decide so quickly, as she had plenty of time in life to develop these decision-making skills.

She was like the little momma of the family. Mikaella kept her cell phone to her ear all the time. One time she was in her room when I tried to get her to come to the dinner table for supper. She delayed coming to supper since she was on her phone, so I called her from my cell phone. It was an unlisted number. When she answered it, I said, "It's time to eat. We are waiting on you."

We both thought this was funny. She was always so well behaved and mature for her age. She immediately came down to dinner with a smile on her face. She also liked music and always had an iPod in her possession. Mikaella had a passion for horses from the time she was a little girl. She dreamed that someday she would have her own horse that she could ride and care for.

Brittany was fourteen years old, and she was a sporty, fun person who liked to play with Trudy's basketball and skateboard around the house. She loved to talk and enjoyed interacting with people. Everything Brittany did, she did with passion and with confidence. She loved her puppy dog, Sophie, and cat, Big Kitty. Brittany had big beautiful blue eyes that looked like a bright blue ocean and a radiating smile that captured everyone's heart. One Saturday, the family went to an air show in Atlanta. The "Blue Angels" were there with their jets and helicopters. Trudy had to scold Brittany occasionally for wandering from the group in the midst of the masses. She came over to me and said, "Everyone is on my case, Papa Ray." She then gave me a big hug, and I told them to be nicer to her. She liked my protection and this made me feel 100 feet tall.

Brittany was a curious girl. She always asked questions, but sometimes she didn't know if they were the right ones to ask. I listened to her questions because I enjoyed answering them. She was an intelligent person. She passed all her classes and was never afraid to share her opinion, and social studies was her favorite class because she loved to debate. Brittany made friends with all different types of people because she truly listened to them when they spoke. Her sensitivity and compassion for others spilled over into every aspect of her life.

We also had a grandson named Kyle who was eighteen years old. Kyle was the color of Trudy's life. She thought he had hung the sky. Kyle was in college studying pharmacy and made the dean's list the first two years he was there. He was tall and slender like me with a keen sense of what he wanted out of life, even as a fifteen-year-old. One year Kyle came with me on a mission trip to Montana to an Indian reservation. I saw Kyle give a young man his coat as he ministered to him. This impressed me, as I thought to myself, *This young man will grow to help many people and be very successful at his trade.* The family didn't see very much of Kyle when he was in college. But after he got out of school and started making money, he came home every weekend. Kyle loved to play the drums and play video games. He also liked to deer hunt and harvested as many as three deer in one season. Our family was very close to one another, and we had fun wherever we went.

~ 7 ~

A Typical Day at the Office

I practiced dentistry in a small town about two hours from Atlanta, close to interstate I-85. I started out by practicing pediatric dentistry at four of the local health departments. I would see as many as twenty-five children in one day and enjoyed interacting with young patients because they were so honest and forgiving. One time, I had fifteen children to see, all in one morning session, and it was their first dental visit. They were all nervous and unsure who I was and didn't want to open their mouths for examination and treatment.

I picked out a little, confident, four-year-old boy who was laughing and talking. His name was Russell. I asked Russell if he would like to be the first one to have his name carved in his shiny filling and then get a surprise gift. I said that I only had a few left, and didn't have enough for everyone, but thought Russell might want to be the first to make sure he got his gift. Russell said he wasn't sure, so I called him to the side and asked him if he would like to be a "hero" today. Russell said, "Yes, I like heroes." I told Russell that if he helped me with his treatment that I would make him a hero and everyone would cheer for him. Russell looked into my eyes and saw that I was serious. Russell took me up on it. Russell's tooth was restored with silver filling in his baby tooth, with all the other children watching every move. He loved the attention, as I carved his name into the silver filling and showed it to him. Russell thought this was the coolest thing he had seen in a while. When we completed the procedure, I told everyone to cheer for Russell, because he was afraid at first, but conquered his fear and finished the procedure. All of the kids clapped and cheered for Russell. Russell had the biggest smile on his face as his peers celebrated his courageous behavior. His lip was numb from the anesthesia, and his smile was half drawn, but he was certainly smiling on the inside. Russell looked at me as the crowd honored him as if to say, "Yes, Dr. Ray, today I am a hero; I did the right thing." After Russell's experience, all of the other children were fighting to get in line to be the next hero. It was a small riot to say the least. Russell was a hero in their eyes, and now everyone wanted a silver filling in their tooth and their name placed in it, whether they had a cavity or not. They cried if they didn't have what Russell had.

It seemed that most children wanted what other children wanted and they enjoyed being "The Hero." I thought this desire was common for adults as well. I believe that most of us as adults also want to be "The Hero." Sometimes a dental procedure could inadvertently inflict pain during treatment when disease was present. After treatment, when asked for forgiveness, adults would usually take a while to forgive the practitioner for the discomfort associated with the procedure. However, children on the other hand usually look the doctor in the eye and with a tear say, "Yes, I forgive you," and they usually mean it. I respected this attribute in children and treated them with respect and honesty. I enjoyed the children and the fun they brought into the office.

After a few years, my practice grew, and I acquired my own dental building. I enjoyed the additional room and freedom to practice with flexible working hours. Initially, I worked six days a week. After a few years, I reduced my days in the office to five days a week, and then down to four days a week. I found that I could be more productive and passionate, practicing well rested and clear minded.

Working five days a week sapped my energy and left me feeling empty. After careful consideration of the work schedule, I found that a four-day week was the right amount of clinic time to treat patients. This gave me the fifth day to rest and Saturday to take care of errands, most of which were on paper, or on Trudy's honey-do list.

It was obvious from my previous training and interests that I liked the technical side of dentistry. I was one of the first dentists in my region to use such technological advancements like digital radiography, 3D CAD/CAM, sleep dentistry, and laser treatments. Most of these advancements were very expensive endeavors and required a significant amount of continuation education seminars, conferences, and hands-on training courses, which usually were initiated and encouraged by Trudy. She often would have great ideas that were challenging and advanced the practice. Trudy would ask me what I thought about a new procedure or technology, and I would ask her about the cost. Trudy would say, "We will get the money if you agree that it is sound technology and would provide better care to our patients." Somehow, Trudy would usually find a way to make things happen.

Trudy enjoyed talking with patients about their families and church activities. The practice was centered on taking care of people, and I liked that.

When one of my patients asked me what I thought about my job, I responded and said, "The profession of dentistry is wonderful and rewarding. I'm not just restoring teeth, but treating a person with feelings and emotions."

Assisting a patient with a dental problem could be very difficult, especially if he or she had a dental phobia. Many patients harbored fear of pain as a result of a previous bad dental experience in their childhood, which reflected dentistry's image in the past. The image of dentistry once viewed as "the torturous dentist leaning over the patient while haphazardly pulling a tooth as the patient yelled in terrible pain" was over and, fifteen years later, looked completely different with dramatic improvements. Modern dentistry, likewise, offered technological advancements with clinicians who were highly skilled and cared about their patients and were ready and willing to help those who suffered with past bad dental experiences. In addition, advancements such as medications that provided comfort sedation or sleep dentistry, laser dentistry that provided drilless procedures without the need for "The Shot," modern anesthetics that provided profound anesthesia, and preventive dentistry which intercepted the disease process before it progressed to advanced stages of pain and suffering—all played a part in making "the dental experience" a better one for the patient.

I enjoyed talking and working with other health-care professionals and discovered after several years of interacting with them that most were respectable and caring people. Most dentists I encountered over a period of many years were compassionate and treated their patients with dignity and respect.

Dentistry was even more rewarding for me than I had originally thought it would be. I wanted to contribute to improving the image of dentistry in some way. My desire was to help the public discover that dentistry was an important and compassionate profession that improved the quality of life.

A typical day at the office could be quite hectic. For example, Trudy would get up at 5:30 a.m. and listen to the current morning news. I would get up at 6:45 a.m. The family would get ready, and Trudy would take the grandchildren to school and be at the office at 8:00 a.m. Trudy was the office administrator, patient coordinator, and financial coordinator. She would take care of administrative affairs in the morning and delegate duties to the team. In the afternoon, she would work on taxes and payroll and, in between, manage family calls and coordinate the grandchildren's school and activities. She was a very busy person with a lot on her plate. She generally would leave the office before 6:00 p.m. I would get to the office around 7:00 or 7:30 a.m. A team huddle would take place where patient acknowledgments would transpire for about fifteen to twenty minutes. For example, a team member might say, "Mr. Jones is coming in today. He is a needle phobic with diabetes. The session will be hard for him because he discovered last week that his mother has breast cancer. We need to be especially compassionate and listen to him talk if he needs to."

The team would take their designated posts and follow the protocol that Trudy and I had written for that day. I would start treating patients at 8:00 a.m. I would have two hygiene patients to examine and interact with, along with two restorative patients, with the possibility of two emergency patients in the same hour.

On one morning in September, I was performing a fixed bridge dental procedure. As I was preparing the teeth, the patient, whose name was Tina, started crying. I asked her if the treatment was causing her discomfort. Tina said, "No," but I knew she needed to talk. I listened as she told her story. Her husband had just lost his job, and their family was feuding with her mother-in-law, who was living with them after being diagnosed with heart failure. Tina was trying to tell me this, and I was trying to understand her emotional crisis, so I could help her cope to endure the dental procedure. Before Tina was able to finish telling me about her situation, the front-desk assistant came to the clinic and informed me that my house had a severe water-pipe break, and water was going into the basement at a rapid rate. Before I could ask Trudy to call a plumber, a patient, who had just left the office, came back into the office and said that he had backed into my car as he was pulling out of the office. While dealing with the emotionally distraught patient, the plumbing problem, and the wrecked car, yet another problem arises. The hygienist signals for me to come to the hallway. Her patient was refusing the x-rays she desperately needed. It was obvious from the initial examination she had severe periodontal disease and would lose her teeth if she refused the treatment. I had no choice but to deal with this dilemma. I spent several minutes with the woman answering her questions, explaining the disease process, and securing her permission for treatment.

Before I could collect my thoughts, another hygienist emerges from room five and informs me that her patient has consecutive appointments and must be evaluated immediately because she has another appointment in thirty minutes and has to leave. On an attempt to examine her, she continues to complain about her son and husband's appointments the following week. She wants to know why her son can't be seen on Tuesday with her husband to avoid two trips.

Meanwhile, another phone call comes in from a specialist. The biopsy results are in for one of our young male patients. The lesion is malignant. The man is in the reception room unaware that he is about to receive devastating news. I was emotionally weary and needed a break, but there was no time. I reach for the intercom communicator to call Trudy and laugh at the chaos. Trudy then calls the plumber. I calmed Tina, quickly solved the issues for both hygienic patients, and quickly got back to finish Tina's treatment in order to initiate treatment on the next restorative patient.

As lunchtime approached, I discovered that there were two computers down that interfered with the taking of radiographs and required immediate attention. Lunchtime turned into another work session. The computer technician and I began working together to find out if the problem was software or hardware related. The problem seemed small at first glance, but needed to be resolved before the next patient came in within the hour.

With so many stimulating events, many coming at the same time throughout most of the day, I often was drained and tired. The efforts were gratifying and rewarding, but came with a price.

All of the patients needed to be taken care of before 5:00 p.m. in the afternoon since there was a three-hour chamber of commerce leadership meeting at 5:30 p.m. The meeting would drain what little emotional and physical resolve I had left. This dialogue and interaction with people in my community was important because I knew most of them personally and had treated them and their children and stood beside them in life and death events. I was usually lucky if I got home by 8:00 p.m.

When I finally arrived home, Trudy was waiting for me at the door. Being married to the office manager had inherent advantages and disadvantages. Trudy wanted to talk about the team meeting scheduled for the next morning. The last thing on my mind was work. This particular team meeting that Trudy was talking about was going to be difficult. During the previous week, one of the team members had a conflict with two of the other team members. The situation was festering and needed to be resolved before it spilled over into patient care. Working in a confined space with so many different personality types could be challenging at times but was definitely worth the effort. Our team understood our vision for the practice and our commitment to the local community as well as our global interest through foreign missions. Two weeks out of every year, the team would pitch in and donate their time to a mission's project. Sometimes the project would involve a local nursing home, an addiction-recovery ministry, or a dental clinic for those less fortunate. Other projects included preparing dental and medical supplies for foreign mission trips that were planned by the church. These projects were a great morale booster for the team since they all shared the common desire to help people in need.

~ 8 ~

Medical-Dental Mission Trips

After a few years into my practice, I was talking to Dr. Jack Moncrief, a dentist in Athens, who was scheduled to go to Peru on a mission trip. Jack had to abort his commitment to the trip, due to kidney-stone problems, and was scheduled for surgery the week of the trip. He told me that I should consider going in his place since he was unable to go because of his illness. At that time, I had never been outside of the southern United States, much less outside the country. After I meditated, prayed, and talked with Trudy about it, I decided to take the challenge. It would turn out to be one of the best decisions that I would ever make in my life. So I agreed to go to Peru to treat patients there. It changed my life forever. The children there had never seen any kind of doctor. After anesthetizing their pain, many of them would fall asleep, due to the immediate relief that the Novocain provided. Their little bodies would just go limp once they were pain free. The people were so kind and generous and had absolutely nothing but a piece of clothing. They had very little food, limited clean water, and no medicine, but they were content and mostly smiling. The Peruvians expressed a deep sense of happiness in spite of their circumstances, which impacted my perspective on life.

This sense of happiness seemed to exist on a global scale with people from different places all over the world. Once, I had an opportunity to take a dental mission trip to Bolivia, South America. A team of fourteen of us flew into Santa Cruz and from there took a bus to Cochabamba. We then boarded a boat and went up the river toward the Amazon Basin about thirty miles until we docked at a small village deep within the jungle. Approximately 200 children would flock to the village during the rainy season for school. The school was very small and there were few books. The children's ages ranged from five to eleven years of age, most of whom had little clothing. Many had no shoes and the temperature would often drop into the forties before the morning sunrise. Our team plan was to treat all 200 children within the five days we had there while in the village. Although the little ones had barely anything to keep them warm at night, no mosquito nets, no medications for sickness, no clean clothes or shoes, they all played well together, slept well together, and did their schoolwork together with little or no quarreling at all during the entire five days we were there. They all seemed to be happy and content with no complaints. One night after treating about fifty of the little patients, I went into their straw-hut home to check on them to make sure they were sleeping well, since I had performed tooth extractions on most of them. I went inside the hut and they were sleeping on the floor with no blankets, in hammocks, and cuddled together to keep each other warm. It was a humbling moment for me to see these little ones sleeping so peacefully, helping one another, and consoling one another. The next morning I rewarded them with a piece of candy since they rarely ever tasted candy, and that afternoon there was a paper trail of candy wrappers that led back to their hut. They were such a joy to treat and were very cooperative to work with as patients.

After taking several mission trips to other countries, I realized that my priorities had gotten out of order, so I started to think about what was really important to me, like the people in my life and how I was spending my time.

What I once thought was important wasn't so important anymore. Taxes, payroll, business overhead, long work nights, unfriendly patients, and bills—all once made the top-ten list of my mental priorities. Although I considered these aspects of life important, the mission experience helped me realize that the most important aspect of my life was my faith in God through Jesus Christ. After my faith, I believed that my family, friends, and health were also important. As far as I was concerned, these all entailed the concept of "quality of life." Not just living or existing, but living a balanced quality life was the important thing to aspire to in life. A life with a sense of purpose and high moral values, priorities, and goals were essential components to the balanced life.

I realized that I was blessed and fortunate to be an American. Having traveled around the world and seeing so many different cultures, governments, and living standards, it was crystal clear to me that America was the greatest nation in the world to live in and to have citizenship. Even though there were conflicts of interest where governments were concerned, people in other countries respected American doctors so much that they made painstaking efforts in traveling long distances by foot to be seen by one if the opportunity arose. Most citizens of Third World countries saw Americans as healthy, prosperous, and giving. The United States of America was a strong and prosperous nation. However, this image of America would soon be tested and challenged.

~ 9 ~

The Twin Towers' Attacks

The attack on September 11, 2001, changed the world in many ways. Although it was not the first attack the radical Muslim world had engaged on American soil, 9/11 certainly had the greatest impact upon the world, which I had experienced in my lifetime.

Shortly after 9/11, many across the world felt uncertainty about our national security and feared the possibility of future attacks. The national security of our nation wasn't the only aspect the world was concerned about. There also was a global concern about the effects these attacks would have on our economy, especially since America was already struggling with precursors of a recession. The attacks hit two symbolic structures in America: the World Trade Center, which represented America's economic complex, and the Pentagon, which was a symbol of America's military powers. The fall of the World Trade Center sent the Wall Street stock trade to a halt for four days and from there went into a whirlwind mode for the next week and took months to show even small increments of the slightest recovery. At that time, our economy was already weak and many economists thought this economical injury would tip the American economy into a full-blown recession. Although the stock market eventually picked up momentum, it would take several years or more to determine the full extent of the damage done by the attacks. As far as the American economy was concerned, there were issues at hand that would have an effect on the forecast of the financial health of this country. Namely, factors such as future economic growth, the status of the United States stock market, the level of consumer spending based on the public's confidence in the American financial structure, foreign investment and spending relations with the U.S., and our Government's spending and budget projections would all play a part in the world's eyes to determine if the American dollar would hold its value or decline in weakness. Of course, there have been previous bouts of economical weaknesses in the past such as during the wars of WWI, WWII, Vietnam, and also during the Great Depression when the New York stock market crashed from which the American economy recovered. The U.S. did bounce back from these economical storms and in some ways even became stronger as a result. However, the 9/11 attacks affected the world in a psychological sense that started a cascade effect in so many areas of American life.

There had been recorded terrorist attacks all over the world such as the Wall Street bombings in 1920 that killed forty people, the Munich Olympic attack that killed twelve people in 1972, the Scotland Pan Am bombing that killed 270 in 1988, a previous attack on the World Trade Center in 1993 that killed six people, the Oklahoma City bombing that killed 168 in 1995, the U.S. Embassy bombing in Tanzania and Kenya that killed 225 people in 1998, the U.S. attacks on 9/11 that killed approximately 3,000 people, the Indonesia bombings that killed 202 people in 2002, and the Madrid bombings that killed approximately 190 people in 2004.

The 9/11 attack was personal since it involved the deaths of so many Americans as well as people who were from all parts of the world and done so in what I called the heart of America, New York. Also, it was a process of destruction, happening over a period of hours with video horror coverage of moment-by-moment footage showing the buildings on fire and eventually one of the buildings collapsing, followed by the second building collapsing. I remember exactly where I was and the time of day that it took place. I was practicing dentistry, and Trudy came back to the operatory and told me that she needed to see me to tell me something, plus it was an emergency. I could tell that she looked upset and concerned, but I didn't know what the problem was. When she told me that the Twin Towers had been struck by a plane, I thought at first that perhaps it was an accident. She said that the media believed that terrorists might have been involved. My heart sank as I heard her speak of the incident. Listening to the news, I realized that terrorists were flying planes into the Towers, and at that point, I experienced a feeling of disbelief and sorrow.

~ 10 ~

The Koran and the Muslim Radicals

It seemed that the radical Muslims were the "giants of terror" of this world. Their quest in life was to take down the "infidel," especially the American infidel. These heartless, deceived, and evil terrorists valued human life as null and void and thought that if someone didn't convert to their way of belief with their interpretation of the Koran, they were considered infidels and should be removed from the Earth. Many have since questioned the Koran and its interpretation to its regard for life of those outside the Muslim faith. One doesn't have to be a scholar to see that, according to the Koran, an infidel is anyone who is not a believer of the Islam faith.

I began to research the different aspects of the Islam faith to learn more about the religion and its practices. Its origin began in the book of Genesis when Abraham had two sons, Isaac and Ishmael. Ishmael was conceived by Hagar, Abraham's bondservant, which was customary and proper for the culture of that time. Isaac's mother on the other hand was Abraham's wife, Sarah.

The Koran speaks of Jesus as only a prophet, as it does Ishmael as well, as noted in 5:75 – "Christ, the son of Mary, was no more than a messenger like the messengers that passed away before Him. His mother was a woman of truth. God makes His signs clear to them, yet they are deluded away from the truth."

The biblical Scriptures state in the book of John to "test the spirit."

> 1 John 3:24b–4:6
>
> *And by this we know that he abides in us, by the Spirit which he has given us. Beloved, do not believe every spirit, but test the spirits to see whether they are of God; for many false prophets have gone out into the world. By this you know the Spirit of God: every spirit which confesses that Jesus Christ has come in the flesh is of God, and every spirit which does not confess that Jesus Christ has come in the flesh is not of God. This is the spirit of antichrist, of which you heard that it was coming, and now it is in the world already. Little children, you are of God, and have overcome them; for he who is in you is greater that he who is in the world. They are of the world, therefore what they say is of the world, and the world listens to them. We are of God. Whoever knows God listens to us, and he who is not of God does not listen to us. By this we know the spirit of truth and the spirit of error.*

Since the Koran as well as the Islam faith did not consider Jesus as the Christ Messiah, the son of God, the Islam faith was the spirit of the antichrist, according to biblical Scripture. Christianity and Islam were opposite one another and had conflicts since early biblical times. The Bible carefully identifies the family tree of Jesus, starting from the beginning of time in the book of Genesis. However, that is not the case with the Islam faith and Mohammed.

The Koran does not have any genealogical records, and the Arabs passed down their genealogies from only their memory. It was surprising to discover that both the Jewish and Islam faiths consider the Arab people to be the descendents of Ishmael.

Furthermore, I learned that the Islamic faith considered the Koran as the divine scripture and that this book was revealed to Mohammed by the biblical archangel Gabriel.

Mohammed was born in Mecca where his father and mother died early in life and left him as an orphan to be raised by his grandfather who died shortly after his adoption and then spent the remainder of his childhood with his uncle. After Mohammed married his first wife, she died after giving him six children, two of which died at an early age due to disease. At age 63, Mohammed became ill with a fever and died.

Mecca has been the center of the Islamic world. It is believed that Mohammed received his vision close to Mecca, where the Muslims gather to worship. Mecca is located in the Sarat Mountains of central Saudi Arabia and is referred to as the land of Hijaz, which means barrier. The land has geological barriers of volcanic mountains and landscaped depressions. Saudi Arabic law is governed by their Koran, which is their constitution and based on Islamic religion. In summary, one could say that the Koran came from Mohammed, a descendent of Ishmael, and claims Jesus to be only a prophet and not The Christ, The Son of God. Neither Islamic nor Jewish faiths believed that Jesus was the Son of God. It was evident to me that the radical Islam terrorists believed that they were serving their god by eliminating the infidels who were not of their faith. It fact, Jihad is an Islamic term that denotes a religious duty for Muslims. The word Jihad means struggle and holy war and appears several times in the Koran. Jihad describes a duty for Muslims to fight and endure the struggle for the well-being of Islam at the expense of anyone who contested Islam.

It was interesting to find that the Christian, Jewish, and Islam faiths all believe in God, Abraham, King David, and even Jesus. But the difference is that only Christians believe that Jesus was the Son of the living God, The Christ. This small but most profound difference made all the difference in the world. That seemed to be the underlying difference that had been the source for war since the division of Isaac and Ishmael.

Not all Islam believers, living by the Koran as their divine book, were "radical" in that not all Muslims "believed" or "interpreted" the Koran to suggest that it approved in the killing of everyone who didn't accept their belief. Some Muslims detested violence and rejected the notion of killing innocent people except in self-defense. It appeared that the "radical" Islam interpreted the Koran with permission to kill innocent people who were not of their belief.

Researching the Muslim faith was interesting yet perplexing to me. It seemed that the more I learned about the Islam faith, the more I realized that the attack on 9/11 was a spiritual attack brought about by the "radical" Islam to eradicate their "infidel" who they chose as the victims in the Twin Towers. This realization angered me greatly. But what could I do about it? I realized that I couldn't resolve a war that had been going on for centuries (Middle East wars between Israel, Iran, Iraq, Afghanistan, etc.), but I felt I had to do something to make a difference. It could be a small difference but, nonetheless, a difference.

I began to pray for what to do next. I prayed about this dilemma for two weeks and told Trudy that the Islamic war was weighing on my thoughts most every day. She said, "Well, then why don't you do something about it—make a difference." I said, "But how—what can I do?" She said, "Do what you do best: go over there and help those in need and show them the love of your God." I thought about what she said for several days and continued to pray for what to do.

The next week Trudy came to me and said, "I was talking to one of our patients today, and their church has contacts in Jordan who need medical and dental care for the refugees there." As soon as she said this to me, I started to wonder if that could really be a possibility.

It was only a short time later that Trudy and I would have an experience of a lifetime, one that would bring both terror and satisfaction, an event that would impact the entire world.

~ 11 ~

Bin Laden, al-Qaeda, and the Taliban

It wasn't long after the World Trade Center attack that I first saw a photo of one of the men responsible for this terrorist act on the news. The news channel showed a fairly recent photo of a man whose name was Osama bin Laden. I had never heard of this man before, but as I saw his picture, my eyes locked on his eyes in the photo. I stared at his picture on the screen until the news station took it off and went on to something else. I was interested in knowing more about this man: where he came from, what were his beliefs, what were his motives—who was he? I began to research bin Laden and discovered some interesting aspects of his life.

Osama bin Laden, which means Obama, son of Mohammed, son of Awad, son of Laden, was born in Saudi Arabia in 1957. His father was a wealthy businessman and had a close relationship with the Saudi royal family. Bin Laden had several wives and children. He believed that Afghanistan was the only Islamic country in the Muslim world since it was under the rule of the Taliban's leader, Mullah Omar. Bin Laden and Omar were both persistent and desperately wanted to see the U.S. and Israel destroyed for their nonbelief in Islam and support for industrialism. They also wanted the U.S. military forces out of the Middle East.

International antiterrorist task forces had known for some time that al-Qaeda and the Taliban were working together as terrorists. Western counterterrorist officials believed that bin Laden and his key chief associates were protected under the Afghan-Taliban organization and suspected these evildoers were probably settled in the remote Afghanistan-Pakistan border region somewhere in Saudi Arabia. Supposedly, al-Qaeda and the Taliban did not get along very well. Bin Laden had more that forty sons and twenty wives. His fourth oldest son, Omar bin Laden, had fled from his father in 2001 in order to escape his punishment and capture, realizing there was a large price on his father's head. Omar had told officials that the two terrorist parties were separate entities and only tolerated each other in order to accomplish a goal in which they shared, which was to destroy America and what it stood for in the name of Allah. Omar revealed that the two leaders had been arguing about their next large mission to attack London.

Osama bin Laden was the chief al-Qaeda leader, and the chief Taliban leader was Mullah Omar. These two terrorist groups often fought over strategies and plans. Bin Laden was jealous of Omar's independence and was angered that the Taliban had such strong connections and power. He wanted all of the power himself but knew that he needed the help of the Taliban. The Taliban followers were many and were strategically placed throughout the Middle East and Asia. Bin Laden's son, Omar, told reporters that his father realized that he could not defeat or overcome the

Taliban, as he knew he would be overpowered and outnumbered. Omar said that his father's personality was strong and capable of withstanding the difficulties of living in the caves in remote mountains. He said that bin Laden's personality was so strong that he thought he could adapt to almost anything in life since his father believed that he was on a mission for Islam and placed himself around his followers who would quickly die for him.

In the year 2000, bin Laden was the head leader in planning the triple attack on Jordanian soil. The attack was planned to bomb the Radisson Hotel in downtown Amman, tourists at Mount Nebo, and on the Jordan River. His planned attack failed when the Jordanian terrorist cell was located and several arrests were made.

In 2004, bin Laden, after initially denying the claims against him for being responsible for the attacks on 9/11, admitted and claimed responsibility for the terrorist action:

> "Allah knows it did not cross our minds to attack the towers but after the situation became unbearable and we witnessed the injustice and tyranny of the American-Israeli alliance against our people in Palestine and Lebanon, I thought about it. And the events that affected me directly were that of 1982 and the events that followed—when America allowed the Israelis to invade Lebanon, helped by the U.S. Sixth Fleet. As I watched the destroyed towers in Lebanon, it occurred to me to punish the unjust the same way (and) to destroy towers in America so it could taste some of what we are tasting and to stop killing our children and women.
>
> "I am the one in charge of the nineteen brothers ... I was responsible for entrusting the nineteen brothers ... with the raids." [5-minute audiotape broadcast, May 23, 2006]
>
> —Osama bin Laden

After 9/11, bin Laden was marked as "the most wanted man in the world" for his evil deeds, and the U.S.A. declared war on terror to remove the Taliban régime in Afghanistan and arrest the key members of al-Qaeda to help prevent future threats of terrorism in the U.S.A. The CIA made changes within its department of Special Activities Division to focus on tracking down and capturing bin Laden, dead or alive.

Bin Laden was indeed on the FBI and CIA most wanted list. However, he couldn't be located. His stealthlike movements remained unseen by international government intelligence as well as by U.S. military intelligence. The caves and caverns in the rocky terrain located within the Middle East made it difficult to locate him.

As America declared war on terror, Saddam Hussein was also on the most wanted lists. Like bin Laden, Hussein's close associates kept his whereabouts top secret. He could also hide in the rocky terrain of the countryside. However, Iraq was about to be invaded by the American troops and could search the entire country to hunt him down. The U.S. troops had no intention of invading Saudi territory, where bin Laden was supposedly hiding; thus, they had limited access to perform a thorough search of the area to pursue him.

Although bin Laden and Saddam Hussein were terrorists on the run, they were well hidden, but for how long? It was a matter of time before the two of them had to show up somewhere and be captured.

In 1991, bin Laden and Saddam Hussein met and agreed on a common quest: to destroy America. They both shared the view that America was a great threat to the Islam world.

Hussein was a dictator who ruled by military force. Bin Laden on the other hand was a "behind the scenes" ruler who led his mission by underground Islamic radicals, namely the al-Qaeda.

Although the two terrorists engaged in different methods of terror and at times had extreme conflict with one another, they vowed to work in harmony without destroying each other. Bin Laden instructed al-Qaeda to not interfere with Hussein's government.

Bin Laden and Saddam Hussein began an operational relationship in the early 1990s that included development of weapons of mass destruction, logistical support for terroristic activity, and explosive training exercises. Bin Laden wanted to expand his organization in Iraq since the country was a safe haven for al-Qaeda.

With such turmoil within its borders, Iraq became a place of fear and death for many of its citizens. As a result, thousands of Iraqis fled the country to escape death and torture. Most refuges fled to Jordan since it seemed to be the most stable country in the Middle East. This mass influx of Iraqi refugees posed a burden on Jordan's government. Government officials of Jordan were unsure as to how to handle or what to do with so many refugees.

~ 12 ~

Ray Reveals the Mega Experience

In June of 2002, Trudy learned of a mission opportunity through Judy, one of our patients. A dental team would be going to Jordan to treat the Iraqi refugees as they fled Iraq into Jordan during the American Iraqi invasion to overtake Hussein's régime.

I looked into the risks and discussed it with Trudy. She had participated in other missions of this type. With her background in nursing and her love for people, she didn't even have to think about it. She said, "Yes, Ray, let's do it."

I began to consider the medical-dental mission trip to Jordan to help those fleeing from the same dark radical Muslim spirit that targeted the Twin Towers. Perhaps in this way I would help show love and forgiveness to a people of religious beliefs different from my own. I realized that helping these people wouldn't solve the world's problems, but it was a start: it was an action—it was *something*.

Trudy contacted the medical doctor in Jordan that was an American missionary living in Amman. Judy and her family had been practicing medicine in Jordan for seven years and knew the territory very well. Judy was the contact person. She knew of a prominent dentist in Jordan that was a "believer" who went to her Christian church in Jordan. Judy told Trudy that the area was in desperate need of medical supplies and that the dental needs were insurmountable. Judy was so excited about the prospect of our coming to provide care to the needy people in that tragic area. She said, "The Jordanian government permits Christian churches and their worship, as long as their faith remains inside the building. Witnessing on the streets or outside the church is forbidden."

Again, I did my homework and studied the plan to execute the trip to Jordan and begin preparation. I had local support from the churches within the community. My best friend Lee was a big supporter and told me he would provide the supplies we needed. I obtained a portable "MASH Unit" containing dental surgical equipment, dental hand pieces and unit, implant armamentarium, anesthesia supplies, as well as miscellaneous supplies. We would be prepared to perform a myriad of procedures from the simplest dental cleaning to the most complex dental surgery with artificial bone augmentation and implant placement. I obtained a portable air compressor and gas-fueled electric generator. I had a case of latex gloves, surgical attire, and battery headlamps that provided bright light during treatment. I had disposable scalpel knives, sutures, and all the necessary dental surgical instruments. I also had a permit from the DEA to take medications out of the country, including narcotics for pain control, antibiotics, anti-inflammatories, and antimicrobial mouth rinses. Of course, my passport was in order with many stamps from other countries and valid for use.

Trudy, the organizer, opened up the office schedule for two weeks and got the plane tickets for Jordan. She called a team meeting. Everyone in the office believed in the mission and assisted the team as they prepared the equipment and supplies they would need for the trip. In all, it took three full busy weeks to prepare. Once all of the arrangements were made, the dental and medical carrying cases were packed, weighed, and ready to go. Trudy and I got up at 5:00 a.m. the next morning and headed to the airport in Atlanta. We flew from Atlanta to London and then had an eight-hour layover at the airport. We then boarded the

"Jordanian Airlines" aircraft, which was an eerie experience in itself. As Trudy and I boarded the plane to travel to Jordan, we were met with about 100 passengers with over fifty percent of them being Muslims, all looking at us, as we boarded the plane. It was really weird having fifty or sixty Muslims with head turbans looking at you like you are crazy. It was as if they were thinking that we must be either crazy or very courageous, and they didn't quite know which. Once we were seated and the plane took off, I reclined my seat and breathed a sigh of relief.

As I rolled my head back on the headrest trying to get comfortable, I saw an Iraqi passenger to the right of me. He looked sick and his body looked swollen. He appeared to be in physical distress, but maintained his composure. As I glanced back at him, I began to think about something that one of the CIA agents and I had discussed a while back. For the past year or so, I had stayed in touch with the CIA to update discussions about the Mikecrodent device and the specifics of the technology once or twice a year. The previous year, I had heard on the news that some of the al-Qaeda members were ill with diabetes and dental problems, which had been discovered during interrogation reviews with captured members. I knew that diabetes increased the risks for dental problems, including infection and tooth loss. I questioned the CIA about this, and they confirmed that their sources confirmed the accuracy of the report.

As I sat in the passenger seat with Trudy to my left, I wondered if the man to my right could be an al-Qaeda member. I could not control my imagination; my thoughts were racing. I started praying. Soon a sense of calm came over me. As I gazed mindlessly out the window, I could see that we were approaching Jordan. My mind immediately turned to the days in elementary school when I would recite the Pledge of Allegiance. At that moment in a childlike inner voice, I recited the pledge. "One nation under God." How wonderful our country is! How fortunate Trudy and I are! I thought about my accomplishments. After my appearance on *The Today Show*, everyone knew my name. My advancements in implant and dental anesthesia techniques and more specifically the Mikecrodent chip had catapulted me into the world of public scrutiny. I was not totally comfortable in the spotlight, but the media exposure afforded me the opportunity to educate the public on dental health and the advancements that were being made in the field of dentistry. This was satisfying to dwell on, and I soon went off to sleep until the flight attendant asked me if I wanted dinner.

We arrived safely into Amman, Jordan, and met Judy at the airport. She was so happy to see us. A cab was waiting. We went straight to our hotel. Judy left us for the night to rest and recover from jet lag and culture shock.

The next morning Trudy and I were still battling jet lag and had as much coffee as we could stomach. After talking with Judy, we were set to start clinic the next day.

On the first day of clinic, several Iraqi families came to the clinic for treatment. The first patient was a lady named Imad. She was fifty years of age and lived under the régime of Hussein for many years. She needed dental treatment almost as badly as she needed medical treatment. She had left everything she owned and now had nothing but her freedom. She said, "My freedom was worth the sacrifice." I asked, "What can we do for you?" Imad replied, "I have a tooth that is paining me on the left side of my jaw." While examining her, I found a badly decayed tooth. It was in her best interest to have it removed.

There was a great demand for treatment in the clinic. Even though we had several members on the dental team, our actual treatment time was limited. I thought back to those hectic days in the United States when everything that could go wrong had. Those days were easy compared to a single hour here. Most of the patients had serious dental problems from years without seeing a dentist.

As Imad was being anesthetized, Trudy and I began to talk with her through an interpreter. She began to thank me on behalf of her country. I told her that most Americans loved the Iraqi people who were peacemakers and that we came on behalf of our country to be of service and help in any way we could. I asked her this question: "If I could bring back a message to America from you, what would you like to tell the American people?"

She said, "Tell the American people that most Iraqi people are peace loving. We disapprove of Hussein's rule, love America, and what it stands for. Tell the people of the Church, that we believe God is coming back soon and that we all should be ready spiritually."

As she spoke, she began to tear up. She also told me that much of what she had learned about America came from *Reader's Digest* magazines. She loved to read them when she could get them. But as soon as the Iraqi government found out about it, they came and took them from her. Although they were able to confiscate most of them, she was able to save a few by burying them in her backyard in plastic bags. When needed, she would dig them up and reread them or share them with friends. We removed her tooth without event. She was grateful. I told her that science had documented research which indicated praying would reduce postoperative discomfort and increase the speed of healing time. I asked if she would like for me to pray for her. She quickly and without reservation said, "Yes, please do."

This was my prayer for her…"LORD, we thank you that you have safely removed Imad from harm in Iraq. Thank you for this surgery going so well without complications. Thank you for strengthening her immune system and speeding her recovery time. Thank you for blessing Imad and her family and for protecting them in times of war. Thank you, LORD, for being with Imad as she seeks your love and statutes. In Jesus' Holy Name, Amen."

She smiled and said, "May God bless you. Thank you so much."

The next patient was an eight-year-old boy from a family of four. The entire family was in the clinic, eager to see what treatment was available for them. The mother stated that the little boy had a dental infection that caused facial swelling and severe pain. She said he would often fall asleep crying from the pain. Upon examination, I immediately found the problem: an abscessed tooth that required surgical removal. As I started, I heard the loud Muslim chanting. It was disconcerting to hear such religious praying infiltrating the entire clinic. As I was treating the little boy, I had his head in my lap between both hands, and I just started praying silently to God in Jesus' name. I prayed the entire time I treated him, as the Muslim chanting continued outside the building with penetrating effects. It was as if two wars were taking place in the spiritual realm. On the outside was the Muslims' Allah god and on the inside there was God the Father, Son, and Holy Ghost. At brief intervals, the chanting would cease, then resume. The chanting was ever present. Trudy and I never got accustomed to it, nor did we let our guard down. It penetrated the air across the entire country. Day in and day out—day and night, 24 hours a day, every month, all year long.

After a few days of intense clinic, Trudy and I wanted to get out and see the sites. Judy, however, didn't think that traveling around the country alone was wise. She reminded us that the local media had picked up our story. In addition to clinic, I was sharing the Mikecrodent technology at the Jordanian Medical University. I was also going to give a presentation there about dental lasers and implants. It was not the big news in Jordan, but the media had covered it. I had opponents in the United States and knew the adversaries here might be plotting our deaths. Judy knew that some of the radical Muslims would want us dead since we were recognized Christian missionaries, helping the Iraqi people who were resisting the rule of Hussein. It was a volatile and hostile time. In less than two weeks, American troops were planning to invade Iraq.

Judy pleaded with us not to go. "Ray, it is Ramadan. You don't understand; it is a sacred time for the Muslims when they fast and do no work. You are placing yourselves in imminent danger."

In retrospect, I should have listened to her, but I refused to submit to their religious practices. I was well aware of their customs, but everyone we encountered treated us with respect. I felt safe in our choice to tour the area's historic sites. Trudy and I wanted to see Petra, a beautiful city in Jordan carved totally out of stone. The entire city is completely rock, hence the name Petra means "rock."

Two days earlier, an Iraqi urologist invited Trudy and me to have dinner with him. We cleared the excursion through Judy. A prominent doctor in the community, he stirred our interest in going to see Petra. He showed us several breathtaking photos of Petra. Before we left, he assured us that we would be safe. I was reluctant at first, but his reassurance calmed my fears.

After three days of clinic, we were exhausted and ready for a break. We rented a car and took off with some food and water and a map. The three-hour drive went by fast. Trudy and I talked the entire way about the people we had treated, specifically the children and their unfathomable happiness in the face of such horrible living conditions. Their young tortured lives experienced so little joy. They had seen the bloody horrors of war, mangled bodies, unending gunfire, bombs, desolation, thirst, starvation, and unimaginable torture. They had seen their parents killed trying to shield them from enemy fire; the innocence of childhood stolen from them.

The weather was cold that day, about 50 degrees Fahrenheit. It was overcast and foggy at times with only a slight wind blowing. Since we had traveled so far and had planned to swim in the Dead Sea, we decided to go swimming in spite of the fact that it was probably too cold. The Dead Sea is different from all of the other great bodies of water due to high salt content. Nothing can live in it. I was intrigued by the buoyancy factor. A person cannot sink in the salty water. It is amazing to float without effort lulled by the peaceful, gentle, womblike environment. We stayed for two hours. I think Trudy enjoyed it the most since she couldn't swim, so this was a real treat for her. When we got out of the water, the sea salt dried to our face like sugar crystals. I emptied one of my water bottles and filled it with water from the Dead Sea to take back to the kids for a science project.

We then planned our route to Mount Nebo, the "promised land" of Moses. From our vantage point standing near the Dead Sea, there were mountains all around us. Roads led up to most of the mountains. The terrain was rugged and stony most of the way. Even the pastureland was rocky. We drove as far as we could to the mountain and walked the rest of the way. We stood where Moses stood and looked out over the great plains and divides with the Dead Sea in the background. Visibility was poor that day, but the view was still breathtaking. I gathered up a few small rocks to take back to the States for my collection. We then headed to a Turkish bath in downtown Amman. The massage and steam baths were wonderful. We stayed there about two hours and headed back to the hotel to gather our things for Petra. We enjoyed the day and felt totally comfortable in our plans to visit Petra the next day. No one bothered us. We were, in fact, mostly alone. During Ramadan, the Muslims remained indoors. There were very few people on the streets or in the stores. The only drawback was that the gas stations and stores were closed, leaving us without access to fuel or food.

Having a full gas tank and extra food and water, we decided to go ahead with our plans to visit Petra.

~ 13 ~

The Abduction

Next on the agenda and plotted on the map was Petra, so we reloaded the camera and headed for Petra. We drove for miles on long, straight roads amidst a barren land.

There was only one paved road to Petra, the "King's Highway." Trudy was driving, and I was noticing the terrain. After a few minutes, I got thirsty and asked Trudy where the bottled water was. It was in the back in the floorboard of the car. I got a bottle and started to drink. The water was cool and clean and refreshing. We never went anywhere without bottled water. I then got the munchies and asked Trudy if she had brought the bag of chips. She started looking around for them as she was driving. The chips were under her legs on her side of the car, so she reached down to get them when suddenly the car swerved. Trudy and I both were reaching for the chips when out of nowhere we heard an ominous scrubbing sound that started underneath the car. I told Trudy to stop the car and pull over. I couldn't take any chances because we hadn't seen any other vehicles for a long time. We stopped the car and discovered that a plastic gas container was stuck underneath, between the axle and the oil pan of the car. The container was empty. Most likely, it had been discarded on the side of the road. The only way to dislodge it was to get the jack and lift the car. I worked quickly to place the jack and had begun raising the car when I heard an unusual sound in the distance. It was a faint sound: "tat tat tat tat." I listened carefully and did not hear it again. As I proceeded to jack up the car, I heard the sound again. This time I was sure it wasn't my imagination. It sounded like a machine gun. Startled, I looked in the direction of the sound but saw no one. I saw only mile after mile of flat, brown, dry, desert land with only a few scraggly trees. Visibility, under those conditions, ranged from fifteen to thirty miles. I finally removed the stubborn container from the axle and threw it to the roadside. Just before I opened the car door to get in, I noticed a reflection, a momentary glint of silver light, emanating from the same direction of the gunfire.

Thoughts of imminent danger sent shivers through me. Without binoculars, I could not determine the source of the light. I did, however, have the digital video camera. If I stabilized the camera on the hood of the car with the zoom focus lens, I could barely make out several black vehicles in the middle of the desert with several men standing around carrying what looked like metal detectors in their arms. We had just passed a mineral mining site, and I figured that they were looking for minerals or something in the ground. It was so far away that I really couldn't be sure what they were doing. At that point, I didn't really care. I told Trudy that it was time to get back on the road. We drove for about forty-five minutes while I started taking photos.

I had forgotten about the men and the sounds I had heard earlier. I had dismissed them as a work detail. Without warning, a small convoy of vehicles appeared seemingly out of nowhere. They were all black with tinted windows. It dawned on me that these vehicles looked similar to the ones I had seen in the distance through the camera zoom lens when we had stopped to remove the gas container from under the car. Leading the convoy was a four-door sedan, followed by a four-wheel drive Dodge pickup truck. There were also two Hummers and two vans. They were approaching very fast. The speed limit in that area was about fifty miles per hour, but these vehicles had to be reaching speeds of eighty to ninety miles per hour.

Mounted on the flat bed of the back of the truck was a large caliber machine gun with a man in a head wrap, holding on to the handles of the gun as they sped by, over eighty miles per hour.

As they passed, I snapped several photos with a bag of chips in the same hand, thinking the bag of chips would camouflage the camera. Trudy warned me to stop. When I dropped the camera to my lap, I saw the men. It was only a glimpse, but a quick glance was all that I needed to identify them as military. They wore masks. The convoy was highly organized and traveling close together.

As they drove completely out of sight, we discussed the details we could each remember about the group, their purpose and identity. We drove for approximately an additional fifteen minutes. We saw no one. Our nerves settled. I stopped shaking. Trudy was still visibly shaken.

Suddenly, in the distance about a mile ahead of us, we saw the convoy again. Coming toward us now, they would soon intercept our vehicle in less than a minute or two. I told Trudy to slow down and let them pass.

Before I had a chance to mentally calculate how long it would take for them to reach us, they were within fifty yards of us. I grabbed for my cell phone and tried to call Judy at the clinic. A few more seconds passed, and they were on us, the guns pointed directly at our faces. The masked men grabbed Trudy and me, then jerked the cell phones away from us. I tried to explain to them that we were tourists and that we were on our way to Petra. They wouldn't listen.

They ignored my explanations and quickly forced cotton sacks over our heads. Next, they took our watches and jewelry. One of the men tried with great force to pull my MCG school ring from my finger. I screamed in pain. My school ring was very tight on my finger, which made it almost impossible to remove without ice and oil lubricant. One of the leaders ordered the guy to stop pulling so hard on my fingers. I was grateful that he didn't injure my hands. I had to protect them, as they were my livelihood of what I did. They did another extreme body search and even checked my boots and Trudy's tennis shoes.

I was reluctant to resist them until they ripped the Star of David from my neck. Trudy said, "Let them have it, Ray. I'll get you another one." At first, her voice projected a level of calm I'd never heard before.

Angered by my resistance, the man hit me with the butt of his rifle. Trudy started screaming. Once again, the man who prevented the guy from ripping my ring from my finger yelled for the attacker to stop hitting me. I found this extremely strange. If they intended to harm us, why would they protect me from injury?

Within seconds, they shoved us into the back seat of the sedan. We traveled off road for over an hour and a half before coming to a stop. I had no idea where we were. I felt only a degree of pain as they transported me to another vehicle. I heard the door open, then another door. We were in a cramped interior compartment of the second vehicle in total darkness, scared to death.

I tried to calm Trudy. She was crying. I told her to stop so that we could discuss our plan of action and decide what we had to do to make it out of the situation alive. I could not grasp what was happening to us. It all happened too fast. We must have driven for at least another day. Being held in the cramped compartment in a fetal position caused severe pain in my back. My muscles ached and my head was throbbing from the head-butt injury. Before long, I was getting severe muscle cramps in my legs. I could not console Trudy. She kept blaming herself. "Judy told us not to come. She warned us. I wouldn't listen. Now, we're going to die here. We'll never see our children again or our grandchildren. They'll never know what happened to us, Ray."

We both thought we were going to die. I lost track of time in the darkness. I had no idea how long we had been locked in, but I had no intention of giving up or going out quietly. While I had no idea of how we might escape our captors, I thought back to the prophecy for the first time. I was told that I would one day face a giant. What if the giant was a metaphor for this situation? What if this was the situation that God intended for me to experience all along so that I could fulfill my purpose? If that were true, then I knew we would be safe. I told Trudy to listen to me. There in the darkness, we found solace in God's promises. I reminded Trudy of the words that were spoken to me years before. With strong faith and God's direction, we would be triumphant over these evil forces. And we began to pray together, hand in hand; we sought God's will.

Eventually, the vehicle stopped. I had drunk two bottles of water before we were kidnapped. I begged them to let me use the bathroom, but to no avail. Instead, we were placed into another vehicle. With the sacks over our heads, I had no idea what was happening. We were totally helpless. When we emerged from the vehicle, neither of us could walk. The cramped compartment and the inability to move for hours had left us partially paralyzed. They had to practically carry us to the next vehicle.

This vehicle drove slowly for several hours. It came to a stop. We waited for what I believed to be two more hours. I finally gave up hope of getting them to let me out to relieve myself. I urinated on myself. I was so embarrassed.

I had bigger issues to worry about, but Trudy, prone to teasing me mercilessly, looked down at my wet pants. A knowing glance and a wicked smile from her let me know that she was chastising me for wetting my pants.

Our next journey would take us out of this car and into a building. There were clues to indicate it was nighttime. The weather was cold, windy, and humid. We could not discern the distance between our departure from the vehicle and our arrival inside a cold room filled with voices. The language was foreign. I knew only a few sentences in their language: *What can I do for you? How can I help you medically? Are you comfortably numb? Please open wide.* I was certain that without an interpreter we would be lost.

Blindfolded and frightened, we sat: I in my urine-soaked blue jeans with Trudy close beside me, thank God. If she hadn't been there, I never could have held myself together. No one spoke to us. Instead, they took us to another room and took our blindfolds off. I saw Trudy's face for the first time since our capture. Her hair looked awful, her face was smudged with dirt and tearstains, but I thought she was the most beautiful thing I'd ever seen. We kissed each other and held tightly, saying nothing until the door opened.

The men who entered wore head wraps and sandals. They had dark hair and facial hair. They were clean, well groomed, and physically fit. Their demeanor radiated self-control and discipline. Communication between them was authoritative. They moved gracefully across the room as if we were not even there. They completely ignored us until one brought us floor mats. We lay down together and attempted to sleep.

Although I was exhausted from the traumatic experience of the life-threatening uncertainty, I prayed most of the night. I prayed for deliverance so that I might fulfill the prophecy. I prayed for Trudy and for our children and grandchildren, and then without a second thought I prayed for our captors. Calm came over me when I finished and waited for God's word. He told me that I was there to be a blessing for the people, especially God's people. I knew that we were here for a reason, or we would already be dead. There was also the haunting memory of the man who would not allow the attacker with the gun to hurt me. Why? It made no sense.

Another twenty-four hours passed. Both of us were starving. When I had almost given up on ever eating again, these two men came in with rice and chicken and tea. We had no napkins or utensils. They did not abuse us or use disrespectful tones when referring to us in their conversations.

Not long after they brought the meal, they returned and completed another body search. I tried to speak with them using the few words I knew in their language, but no one would acknowledge my conversation. They took my wallet and looked at my identification card. Then one nodded and said something to the other that I did understand, "This is the man we wanted."

I was shocked by the comment. *Why would they want me? How could they even know who I am?*

~ 14 ~

Relocation

The next night, they moved us several times. Our heads remained covered. They gently guided our steps. I thought I even heard one of them popping bubblegum. I don't know why, but, in a flash, I remembered that I had a tracking system in my tooth. There was no way for them to take that away from me. I considered the possibility that they knew of the Mikecrodent system through the media, but was confident they wouldn't suspect me to have one attached to MY tooth. Most of the media had centered the attention on the chip's ability to locate missing "children" and hadn't mentioned adult usage. Besides, even if they did suspect that I had a chip placed on my tooth, I knew they didn't have the skills necessary to detect it in my mouth.

A few minutes later, we were taken to a room and x-rayed. The equipment was outdated but functional. Next, they took our blood and fingerprints. For some reason, they even took hair samples. I was not concerned about the x-ray or that it would detect the Mikecrodent chip's presence. The old machine had low-resolution capability. Not only that, it was well hidden, masked in its appearance, and similar to a silver filling.

It would take a digital sensor x-ray with high resolution, at just the right angle for them to spot the device. I could tell they were not skilled clinicians and were very sloppy at their technique of radiography, as if they had learned it online.

For someone to locate me, he had to know the password and login code to activate the satellite. I was the only one who had the access codes. I did show my brother the previous year, late one night, but I wasn't sure if he could remember the code, since we agreed not to write it down. What a mess! I felt a sense of hopelessness again and told Trudy that we shouldn't say anything about the device because they might be monitoring us. As soon as she realized what I was saying, her face lit up. For the first time in several days, she felt hopeful. However, she didn't know I was the only one with the access code. I quickly returned to my prayers.

I could see in her eyes that she was tired and scared. We both wondered about the well-being of the children and grandchildren. Out of habit, we would call them on the cell phone every day that we were away. Without a phone call, they would be worried. If our capture had already been reported, then the world would know we were missing.

Occasionally, we would hear portable radio walkie-talkies sounding off. I was too far away to determine what they were saying, but I did hear part of the last comment—that they were going to see the dentist. I prepared Trudy. Within five minutes, two Iraqi men came in and sat down on the floor with us. In English, they told us that they knew who we were. The older one said, "We know you are a dentist; that's why we took you. We saw you on television. We want you to treat our leader. He has a serious medical-dental problem. He is very sick. If you treat him successfully, we will release you both, unharmed."

He went on, "If you fail, then you will be tortured. Then, we will kill you both. We have connections in America, and we know where you live. We also know where your five grandchildren are in Georgia. You must cooperate with us if you wish to see your family again."

I protested, "How can we be sure you will live up to this agreement? How do we know you will set us free?"

Showing no anger, he said, "You have no choice. You must accept our demands. We have no reason to kill you or your wife—if you do what we say."

Stalling for time, I told him I wanted to talk to my wife first. "You leave us and let us talk." Trudy and I moved toward the corner of the room. "Trudy, we have to do what they say. They'll probably kill us anyway and leave no trace, but what are our options?"

Before Trudy could answer, the man screamed, "Now! What is your decision?"

Trudy and I agreed that we should go along with their demand, if for no other reason than to buy some time until we could figure out our next move. We said, "We agree to treat this special person as you request." I told them that I would provide the most excellent care to this person, provided they release Trudy. I told them her release would alleviate my trembling hands, and that way I could do my treatment with precision hands without the fear and worry of her well-being.

I asked them to return my Star of David necklace, but they refused. They also refused to release Trudy. "Absolutely not," he said. "We know that you two work together. You will need her to complete the request." I argued with them, "No, I do the surgery by myself."

"No—you lie—enough! Do you agree to complete our offer?"

I discerned from the look in their eyes and their body language that they were not interested in my protests. These men were not negotiators and would not take no for an answer. I perceived from their tone of voice that I had crossed the line. They were willing to die for their cause.

I had lost control over the situation, as if I ever had any control to begin with.

This ordeal was wearing me thin. I was exhausted and now about to prepare for a demanding dental surgery that required precision. I told them that I would need the proper equipment. They said that they had already taken our equipment from the clinic location and had set it up for us. No detail was overlooked.

I thought to myself, *There must have been a plan all along, and someone must have helped them within the clinic vicinity.* I asked the men when they wanted us to begin. When they said today, I panicked. "You must help him as soon as possible. He is very sick; we have little time." The man looked worried. I had a bargaining chip now. They needed me. I convinced them that Trudy and I must be well rested and fed in order to undertake such a complicated surgery.

Reluctantly, they agreed. Several minutes passed. They brought food and water for us. Trudy and I were both mentally and physically exhausted by this point. We desperately needed sleep, but we also needed to stay awake to devise a plan of escape or action for negotiating our release. If we could postpone the treatment, rescue might be possible. As long as they need us, we would be allowed to live. As Trudy and I lay there on the dark, cold floor, cushioned only by a thin mat, we came to the only rational conclusion: we had to treat him and trust that we would be released.

I spent several minutes surveying the room we were in. It was probably underground with only one set of stairs and a door barred from the outside. From my estimations, I determined the dimensions of the room in feet to be twelve by twelve. There was a dim light, probably from a gas generator. Occasionally, we saw the lights flicker and sometimes go out. I found candles on a low, wooden table and lit one of them. On the floor etched deeply into the stone were deep scratches, possibly indentations resulting from having dragged heavy objects across the floor. My mind conjured up horrible torture scenes from Edgar Allan Poe's story *The Pit and the Pendulum*. I couldn't entertain these thoughts any longer.

It had to be past midnight. All I could think of was Trudy and her prayer, "I know the plans that I have for you, plans of well-being and good. No weapon formed against you shall prosper." I joined in prayer with her in one voice through "prayer and supplication," making our requests known to God. In this manner, we fell asleep together in each other's arms.

~ 15 ~

Meeting the Giant

We were awakened the next morning by three men we had never seen before. One of them spoke English, very poorly, but we could understand him. He said, "Come with me." They blindfolded us and took us upstairs into another room. We waited for approximately an hour before they removed our blindfolds.

The room was not modern, but it was clean and, to our total amazement, contained all of our medical, surgical, and dental supplies. A generator was brought in to run the equipment. I was in awe of their ability to transport these supplies without being apprehended. It must have taken an incredible amount of time, organization, and research to accomplish such a task in a short period. This man must be very important for them to go to such trouble to kidnap Trudy and me and steal the equipment. These people knew exactly what they were doing, and they were very serious about their mission.

By this time, my neck was stiff and sore. My eyes were so fatigued that I was having difficulty focusing. A gritty, sticky film covered both eyes. I felt the lump on my head where the blood had dried and entangled my hair. Trudy was not faring much better than I. Her hair was sticking straight up in the air. Always the optimist, she said, "Ray, you know I always rise to the occasion, so does my hair." It was not one of her funniest puns, but I laughed anyway.

The men returned and ordered us to begin. We set up the portable dental unit and assembled the surgical instruments as usual. Bowls, disinfectant, and sterile wraps were strategically positioned. I reached for my headlamp. I was surprised to see it was my own from the clinic in Jordan. These men had been meticulous in their preparation of the room.

It took us about an hour to set up, but we did it, and we were ready for any kind of dental problem that came through the door. We told them that we were prepared to proceed when they were. We waited for almost two-and-a-half hours. Then, suddenly, they came over to us and placed the head covers on us again, and soon afterwards, we heard men coming from the other room. As the group of men came into the room, everything fell silent. They took off our head coverings. We both gasped in disbelief. Standing before us was bin Laden himself. He was sitting in the chair with several men surrounding him, including the two men who spoke to us in English. I could barely breathe when I realized the importance of this situation: I am being forced to treat the most wanted man on Earth. Trudy turned to me; we were speechless. I didn't know whether I should speak to him or perfunctorily go through the procedure without interacting with him at all.

The men wanted to get started immediately.

Bin Laden looked terrible. His face was severely swollen on the left side, to the point that his left eye was swollen shut. He looked dehydrated and frail. He still had facial hair, but it had been woven to prevent it from interfering with his treatment.

While the men around him were talking to him, he just sat there looking at me as if to say, "I know by the look on your face you know who I am. Are you going to help me or what?"

Three of the men held rifles as if they were extensions of their bodies. Two dogs followed along closely behind them. When they started to bark at us, the man commanded them to stop. Immediately, the dogs sat. I noticed they wore unusual-looking collars. Upon closer inspection, I detected the presence of a radio device that I had not seen before in the United States. These dogs were obviously well trained. A Rottweiler and a Doberman, they were healthy, sleek, and muscular. I could not, however, ascertain why they would have radio collars.

While we were in the room with bin Laden, I observed one of the men working on a laptop computer. His attempts to secure an Internet connection yielded no results. It obviously had WiFi capabilities, but it was not connecting. I could not imagine why he would be trying to go online. We were underground; chances of reaching a live connection were almost nonexistent. I think he was trying to execute a program. Then, it occurred to me. My Mikecrodent chip was interfering with his computer.

He struggled with it for ten more minutes and gave up. I was relieved until he proceeded to scour the room for signs of interference, potential problem areas for frequency distortion or for a device that might block the signals. He stared at me, twice, and then looked away. Alarmed by the sudden interest he had in me, I returned to the business of examining bin Laden's mouth.

I noticed several times that one of the men in the group kept nodding his head when I would speak. He seemed especially gracious when interacting with me but harsh when he spoke to the other men. They wore black turbans like those usually worn by the Iraqis. I noticed that the man with the red turban was missing a finger on his left hand. I could see it as he wrapped his hand around the barrel of his rifle. I wondered what happened to this man.

Meanwhile, the radio walkie-talkies were going off every few minutes. I hesitated for several seconds before approaching bin Laden. I knew I had to examine him, ask questions, and touch him. I could not begin without finding out about his other health conditions. When I asked him the first question, a simple straightforward question about his general health, the interpreter stopped me. "No. You begin *now*." He was adamant that I had absolutely no interaction with bin Laden.

I asked bin Laden to come over to the dental chair or medical table. He began to try to get up, but was very weak. He required assistance in order to make the few steps across the room. His hair was filthy. He smelled horrible. It was a smell I'll never forget. He smelled of death, decay, pus, and rotten flesh.

As his associates brought him closer to me, my heart began to pound, reverberating through my entire body. I could actually see my shirt moving, and I could count my pulse from the beating inside my head. My adrenalin was pumping hard, forcing my system into hyper-alert mode. I felt as if I were going to explode.

I tried to keep my composure, maintain my professional training, but this was too much for me to bear. The cobra that stared back at me had tortured thousands. He did not deserve my help. I tried hard to control my emotions.

I struggled to stay focused and began to slowly regain my senses as I went back into the flow of the examination. As I touched his cheek to feel for suppleness and fever, it was strange to realize that this was just a man, like any other human being, physically. This man had physical limitations and suffered from disease, as we all do. This weak, frail man was severely ill and immunocompromised as well. His eyes drooped, and his breathing was distressed and shallow. I noticed he had numerous scars on his hands and arms. At first, they appeared to be inflicted by knives because they were long and slender cuts.

When I leaned forward to begin the examination, I had to lift his dirty beard. I found swelling in the neck as well as swollen lymph glands. That's when I noticed he had a gold necklace around his neck. I moved my hands slightly as if to examine another section of his throat. When I did, I found that the necklace was emblazoned with the numbers 911.

At this point, I suddenly realized that I was standing twelve inches from the most wanted man in the world—the man responsible for the deaths of thousands of innocent people. I had no adrenalin left. The fatigue, combined with sorrow and fear and anger, transported me into a nightmarish state of mind. I wanted to take him out, but I knew I would be risking Trudy's life. I distanced myself from the events of the past and focused entirely on the treatment of this sick, old man. I vowed to treat him to secure our freedom.

I wavered back and forth between nausea and disdain as I attempted to seize control of my emotions. I would never be able to pull this off if I didn't.

I immediately turned around and pretended to be looking for something in my dental supply container. I stalled for a short time to gain a modicum of emotional stability. My goal was to stay alive and get Trudy out of this hellish situation. Making eye contact with her helped me refocus. I returned to face this ugly, evil man and asked him to open his mouth. His face was so infected and swollen that he could only open his mouth ten millimeters. A minimum of forty millimeters would be necessary to treat him.

This condition is called trismus, and is due to the infection process called "cellulitis," which inflames the tissues to the point that the muscles and tendons are unable to stretch. The loss of elasticity restricts the jaw's ability to open to a normal width.

Then suddenly an idea came to me. At home in my personal practice, I would place the patient on antibiotic therapy for a week. The swelling and inflammation would be reduced significantly.

I thought to myself, *This is it! This is the ticket we need in order to buy more time, perhaps even another two to five days of time.* Although, I could have sedated him and probably done the surgery under deep sedation right then and there, they didn't know this. Besides, I could show them that he couldn't even open his mouth wide enough for me to treat him. On the other hand, this man might die in his sleep if I don't deal with his infection immediately.

If I sabotaged his medicine, it could kill him, and I would have removed the most wanted man on Earth. Of course, Trudy and I would die, but it was an option. On second thought, it wasn't an option. It would have been an option if I were the only one involved. I could not allow my wife to lose her life in pursuit of my own revenge. I began to pray about what I should do. I decided to demonstrate bin Laden's limited jaw movement and recommend that he receive antibiotic therapy for seven days, knowing that they would likely demand fewer days.

I called the men together and explained why antibiotic therapy was necessary. They rejected my recommendations. I tried to calm them down and get them to listen to the reason for the delay. "No, you must start now. He will die if you delay." They were livid. It was obvious they distrusted me. I told them to Google "dental infection treatment protocol." Arguing among themselves, they turned to me with threats of torture and death if I were trying to trick them. Rejection of my suggestions led me to offer an alternate treatment: a glucose drip and oral antibiotics. I assured them that this protocol would lead to improvement in his condition. Furthermore, I would monitor him closely and begin treatment the minute we saw the swelling went down.

For the moment, bin Laden was not well enough to make critical decisions concerning his care. He was both mentally and physically incapable of ruling in his own behalf. Perhaps, they were keeping him alive because he represented their hero or savior. They championed his cause. They might also be afraid that the al-Qaeda would weaken without him.

I could have given him an IV drip with antibiotics. This regimen would work within a day or two. I was withholding this information until I needed it as a backup in case his condition worsened. Stalling for time might allow the authorities time to find us.

At any rate, they agreed to go with the glucose IV drip and oral antibiotics for now and would look into my recommendations, most likely to check my mendacity. My goal was to buy more time. As we finalized the plan, Trudy began setting up the IV glucose drip and got out the bottles of oral antibiotics. She asked me which medications I wanted to prescribe and administer to him. I said loudly, so the others could hear me, "I want the strongest medication I have available to give. Do you have any Augmentin?" (Augmentin is a brand-name antibiotic that is commonly used in dentistry to treat severe oral infections and is very effective.)

Trudy said, "Yes, we do have it." Of course, I knew we did. I had packed it myself in the green bag. But I wanted to make it appear we were being meticulous in our concern for their leader. Trudy continued to prepare the mini pharmacy we would need.

"Let's give him a seven-day dose," I replied. Trudy counted out the capsules and placed them in a small, brown envelope. She wrote the name on the envelope, the dosage, and the directions for administration: *Take two immediately, then one capsule every six hours.*

When we tried to administer the first two capsules, he resisted. It was a struggle for him to open his mouth wide enough to even swallow. We were forced to open the capsules and mix them with a drink. I'm not certain what it was, but it smelled of alcohol. We asked the men for a straw. They were unable to find one.

Trudy began to search for a vein to start the IV glucose drip. Bin Laden was thin. Finding the vein might be difficult. The stiff, rigid veins of a diabetic patient often roll off the tip of the needle, making penetration difficult.

Trudy chose a vein on his right wrist. She wiped the site with some hand sanitizer that we had in small disposable packets and began to forward the needle. Just as I predicted, the needle would not penetrate. He squirmed and pulled his arm in response to the pain. Several men had been watching our every move. As the men steadied their leader's arm, another vein had blown. The hematoma, which forms from a blown vein, can be serious. I did not react but calmly told them, "Don't worry; this happens sometimes. We just have to put pressure on the site and bandage it." They seemed to understand.

Trudy tried another vein. It went in easily. The IV glucose drip began to flow into his vein. At least, for now, we had appeased our captors. Our actions reassured them that we were competent enough to treat him. For the first time, we felt there was hope that we would be released.

Within thirty minutes, bin Laden began to stir. His eyes were brighter. Trudy and I made loud comments to each other within earshot of bin Laden's men. Our purpose was to encourage them. They had to believe that we could affect this man's survival.

It was soon obvious that the glucose drip was working, because his blood sugar was rising to normal levels. We monitored his vital signs and found they, too, were returning to normal.

Suddenly, the radios blared out a frantic distress call. I thought a bomb was about to drop on us. As it turns out, they couldn't find the straw needed for the patient to sip his medication.

"No problem," I told them, "I'll just make one with a disposable paper tray sheet." Using this homemade straw, he sipped his medicated drink mixture of wine and antibiotic powder. He signaled that he had to go to the bathroom. I told them that this was normal because his body was being rehydrated. In the process, frequent urination occurs. It was a good sign.

They did, however, have a problem moving him. We didn't have an IV bag stand, so they had a man hold the bag up in the air the whole time. This took a considerable amount of discipline. It had to be painful to the man holding the IV bag. It was the equivalent of holding a three-pound bag of bananas for 45 minutes above your head. This guy knew if he lowered the bag, the medication wouldn't drip. He held bin Laden's life in his hands, so he was sweating profusely.

I could see the anguish on the man's face. As the men struggled off to the bathroom with one of them holding the bag neck high, they scrambled across the room like a startled school of fish all trying to go in the same direction, bumping into one another with clumsiness and disorder. Watching their struggle satisfied me in a most awkward but comic way, as I felt no sympathy for these madmen. I silently rejoiced in their difficulty.

They were gone for about thirty minutes, and I began to wonder, *I hope they don't call for me to go back there with him.* Shortly afterwards, a few of the men returned without bin

Laden. At first, I was alarmed, as I wondered what had happened to him. But quickly I discerned from the look on their faces that he was all right. They had returned to orchestrate our next move.

~ 16 ~

The Day after the Dental Evaluation

They bagged our heads again and took us back downstairs to our holding cell. Trudy and I were both exhausted. I could barely hold myself upright, but the minute we reached the room, I felt better. I could talk with Trudy and discuss our situation. We found food on the floor, chicken and bread. It was filthy and covered with horseflies. Normally, I could never stomach a meal contaminated by insects and full of germs, but I was too hungry to whine about that now. As we lay down on the mats, we thanked God for our life together and for His love. I was out like a dead man. I remember waking up in the middle of the night and hearing Trudy snore as if she were gasping for air. I knew she was not in distress. It was that endless snoring. Now, I found her snoring peaceful. I knew she was finally getting some of the rest that she needed. With some food and rest, Trudy's problem-solving skills were amazing.

In the darkness, I listened to Trudy's uneven breathing, but I was unable to doze off. I couldn't get my mind off the children. *Will I ever see them again? Did I let them know how much I loved them? Did I give them my best?* Trudy jerked in her sleep. I wanted to wake her, but I didn't. In the oppressive darkness, I was alone with my shadows. Rather than wallow in my sorrow, I began to pray. In times of extreme loneliness and fear, I prayed that God would take over my thoughts and point me in the right direction. I listened, but for the first time in my life, I could not hear.

I tried to think about what would take place tomorrow and the condition bin Laden would be in, but my thoughts were distorted from the trauma of the day.

I could not even focus well enough to concentrate on a plan of escape. I kept seeing bin Laden's face. I had to keep this man alive. If I let him die, we would die. My professional expertise would be more important in this instance than it ever had been before. I could make no mistakes. I had not even considered the possibility he would die. I had to remain positive for Trudy. I was losing track of the time. I didn't even know what day it was. I couldn't go back to sleep. I stayed awake all the rest of the night—thinking, pondering, and praying.

I guess it was a few hours later when two men came in and wanted to talk. They said that our children were in Georgia with members of their family and that they all were well. I figured they told us this to assure us that they were still in control, and that we were to continue to comply with their mission or "otherwise." They also said that the Americans had invaded Iraq and that several American soldiers had been killed. They seemed cocky and confident and arrogant with a major attitude. I couldn't tell if they were lying or not. If they were not lying, then we had been there about twelve days, based on the invasion date that had been predetermined weeks earlier. I was certain that we hadn't been there that long. This assessment led me to believe that they were just trying to intimidate us, boasting about their strong military capabilities. I asked them about the condition of bin Laden, and they replied, "He is resting in a well-protected safe place where no one can find or bother him." I asked them what they intended to do with us after we had helped their special friend. They said, "We have told you this; why do you ask this thing again?" I asked, "How and when do you…?" They abruptly stopped me and said, "No more! We will go now."

This bothered me, as it seemed they were such organizers and planners, yet they weren't convincing me that they really had a plan to release us. Or, if they did, it certainly wasn't thought out, like the plan to kidnap us was. Or, maybe they had a plan to release us and just weren't going to discuss it. I hoped it was the latter. I wanted to hope for the best so much, especially when I would look at Trudy and think of the kids. But the worst scenario just kept overriding me in my thoughts.

~ 17 ~
The Big Idea

Wait a minute, the microchip! I had been counting on the chip to save us, but there was no way the satellite could receive my signal in the rock cavern. I had also been counting on Judy and the officials at the clinic to report us missing. If she hadn't, we were doomed. Even if my brother remembered the code, it is unlikely the rescue mission would find us in time. My heart sank. I am not one to give in to negative thinking, but the realization came to me: I had the chip technology to bring this giant down. I had a plan, and I slept.

I woke up when I felt the gentle shaking of my wife's hand on my shoulder. I embraced her tightly and whispered, "Trudy, I have a plan. We might not make it out of here alive. I know that now. But we have a chance to change the future. I can implant the chip..."

Before I could finish the sentence, the door flew open. The men commanded us to come. The first thing I noticed was the change in their demeanors. The tone in their voices was harsh and tempered in anger.

They blindfolded us and dragged us to another room. Shortly afterwards, the men came in again with cameras and started taking pictures of us. This was creepy. What were they doing? Would they use them as propaganda to prove that we were traitors, or were we being photographed before we were murdered? For whatever reason, they were calling the shots, so we complied. I had seen these guys get upset before, and I surely didn't want to arouse them now. Things were flowing fairly well at this point. At least we were still alive.

I tried to stop the man with the missing finger. The others ignored me, but this man turned and barked at me, "What do you want?"

"How is bin Laden?"

"He is doing well." I was surprised to find out he spoke some English.

"I need to see him. He is very sick."

"...No, he is not here." Another man came back to bring us food. Finding the first guy still in the room, he yelled at him, probably because he was talking with us.

I told them that this refusal might compromise his recovery and complicate the needed treatment. They confidently said, "That is not possible, as he is far from here in a safe place." We were, once again, blindfolded and taken back to the cold, dark room.

~ 18 ~
The Bizarre Surgery

Approximately two days passed. With each random sound, we cringed in fear. If bin Laden had recovered, they didn't need us anymore. They could have held us captive or killed us. We waited, and we prayed.

Two men burst into the room and ordered us to stand. They placed the head coverings on us, as they had done countless times before. Dragging us back up the stone stairway, they deposited us in a room but didn't remove our head coverings. The two men stayed in the room with us. I heard one of them cough. Then their radios went berserk again. I couldn't understand a word of the discourse, except for the two words "bin Laden."

A few moments later, several men returned. They uncovered our heads. There sat bin Laden. He had recovered from the near-death experience. His color was good. A cursory glance told me the swelling was almost gone. The monster had recovered from his physical storm for the moment, although I knew underneath he was still a very sick man. He was communicating with his men, engaged in animated discussions, pointing toward me, asking questions. Without assistance, he got out of his chair and walked in our direction. Without expression, he said, "I am ready to begin."

I had him sit on the medical table and then lie on his back so that I could examine him more thoroughly. The antibiotics had effectively reduced the inflammation. He could now open and close his mouth, obviously without exaggerated effort or pain. When he opened his mouth, I saw several missing teeth. Root fragments and bony defects indicated he was treated by someone without dental training. I was almost certain he was diabetic and suffering from kidney failure. He had some decay but very little. He also had severe periodontal disease, common in patients who were immunocompromised. On the upper left jaw, two abscessed teeth from the periodontal disease had caused a severe sinus infection with subsequent septicemia. The infection had spread to his bloodstream.

The treatment plan was on track. Now that the infection was controlled, I needed to extract the abscessed teeth. No problem, I could remove the teeth painlessly, repair the sinus perforation, and suture up. I explained the treatment regimen as bin Laden and his men listened. The interpreter repeated what I had told them. They talked for a short time, then turned back to me.

"This is good. But he wants dental implants. He needs them to chew," the interpreter spoke haltingly as if he were trying to recall the words he wanted to use.

The procedure they were requesting was complex and tedious, clearly contraindicated for bin Laden at this point in his recovery. I was almost certain he was suffering from diabetes. The implant site consisted of scar tissue and mushy, partially inflamed tissues adjacent to the sinus perforation. Contraindications included inadequate bone for the implants to set. I told them, trying to explain, but they wouldn't listen.

"Do it." The man standing closest to bin Laden was apparently a man of importance. Bin Laden said nothing.

"I cannot do this surgery. He has no bone to receive the implant. I would need crushed bone particulate for the bone augmentation procedure." I figured this would stop them in their tracks.

Then one of the men said, "We will get the bone; we have access to whatever bone you need to complete treatment."

"How do you have such bone?" I could only imagine which man would have to die to provide the bone.

Without a hint of emotion, he said, "We have a man that will provide it."

I told him the bone would have to be from someone with the same blood type as bin Laden. We did not have access to blood lab facilities or equipment. I told him that we could take bin Laden's two extracted teeth and crush them up into a gritty, fine, sandy powder to use as filler. This was, by far, a much safer substitute. His body would be less likely to reject it. With a compromised immune system, he would not fare as well with foreign tissue. Although this technique had never been attempted in trials in the United States, I thought that at least it might prevent the sacrificial death of a man for his bone tissue. At any rate, they bought it hook, line, and sinker.

Trudy began assisting me with the anesthesia and surgical instruments. After successfully removing the two diseased teeth without complications, I repaired the sinus floor with a Gore-Tex membrane that I had brought along on the trip in the event a patient needed it for a sinus perforation. These membranes are synthetic and expensive. I brought this one along because it was of no use in America. While not ethical for use in the United States, the expired membrane was perfectly safe for use in surgery.

Two men hovered near us, staring over our shoulders, as we placed the Gore-Tex membrane in the exposed sinus floor. I took the two extracted teeth and began crushing them with two flat stones like a mortar and pestle and poured the contents into a clay bowl. I removed the soft necrotic and inflamed pulp tissue from the teeth and retained the hard enamel and dentin granules that had properties similar to natural bone in the jaws. Serving as a matrix for his bone cells to grow into and around, the augmentation material would hopefully facilitate bone growth and stimulation. We then took the bone powder and saturated it with disinfectant and washed the grainy particles thoroughly with the water they had provided. I wasn't convinced the water was sterile, so I heated the clay bowl with a flame to sterilize the solution and removed remnants of any soft tissue tags that might retard healing and inhibit bone stimulation. I filled the socket sites with the bone chips and then placed the two dental implants into the site. I sutured carefully, trying to access only healthy, viable tissue.

The procedure was successful. The surgical site looked good. I was secretly pleased with the job I had done under virtually impossible conditions. I turned to the men with confidence, "It is done; he did very well."

"But there is no tooth showing to chew with." The man was angry. He reiterated, "You give him the teeth now."

I told him this was normal protocol for the implants to osseo-integrate for six months. Only then can the teeth be placed upon them, only when they were solid and nonmovable. I said, "At this point in the treatment, the mushy crushed bone cannot support the weight and bite stress of the tooth part of the implant. If we place it now, it would surely fail in the weeks to come."

They found this explanation to be unacceptable. Their voices grew louder, and the interpreter could not keep up. I was afraid they would kill us if we did not comply. I thought for a couple of seconds, and then asked them to let me talk with Trudy. I assured them we would come up with a solution to the problem.

Trudy and I talked it over. She said, "Just put something on there that looks like a tooth. It doesn't matter what it is, look at these guys, Ray. They're going to kill us. Just do it!"

As she was talking, I thought of an idea that might satisfy them and buy us more time. I told them that I needed two more molar teeth that I could extract from someone else. I assured them that it would pose no health risk for bin Laden since the tooth part was not commonly implanted but rather attached above the gum line. Since the enamel was inert and biocompatible, the issues of rejection do not apply.

I said, "If you bring me a volunteer, I will select and extract the teeth myself. Just get me another patient." I told them this because I figured it might keep them from killing someone to get the teeth that I needed to complete the surgical procedure, and I could perform the surgery with anesthesia, painlessly. The donor would not suffer.

Within ten minutes, they returned with two prisoners. I carefully examined them both. They would not open their mouths at first. I asked the man in charge to make them. I selected the one that had the most teeth. I figured the other guy had fewer teeth. For him the sacrifice would be greater. They both were scared to death because they thought we intended to torture them. From their reactions, I surmised they had already been tortured repeatedly. I tried to calm the "chosen volunteer" but to no avail. He was trembling. One of the soldiers held a gun to his head. He warned him not to move while I anesthetized him. My own heart was pounding uncontrollably. The rifle was only a few inches from my head. Adding to my own fears, the gunman had his finger on the trigger. The poor man was shaking. I was not much steadier. Giving the injection was difficult under these circumstances. I just knew any moment the gun would accidentally go off with this man's head in my hands. Not to mention that the bullet might strike me. I was right up in his face. I had to be, to apply ample pressure to remove the teeth from the jaw. I am certain the patient had no idea that he was providing tooth replacement for bin Laden. Perhaps, he thought that this was some form of insane torture, but had to be puzzled as to why we anesthetized him, and his surgery was so painless. I was almost as horrified as he was during the procedure. I knew he was traumatized because he had soiled his pants. I felt sorry for him since I knew the embarrassment of sitting in one's own urine. Nonetheless, he left there completely and comfortably numb with two fewer teeth than when he came in.

As bin Laden rested on the medical table, I took my dental headpiece and contoured the teeth, as a dental implant attachment or ceramic crown would be shaped. I then drilled a hole in the underneath surface of the crown of the tooth part and placed the customized and handcrafted crowns onto the implant heads and fitted the bite. I placed the two crowns (hand-shaped tooth parts) onto the two abutment attachments that came with the implants. These were stock abutments, standardized but not customized to fit. I just didn't care anymore. No dentist had ever attempted a surgery of this type. All I cared about was getting Trudy and me out of this situation alive. When I was about to give up, a voice inside my head said, "Put the Mikecrodent chip on bin Laden's tooth."

While customizing the teeth for implantation, I looked stumped, intentionally, and placed the handpiece up to my own mouth and began to start it. Trudy shouted, "What are you doing?" This got their attention.

I told Trudy to calm down, that I knew what I was doing. I spoke loudly, so the others could hear every word and told her that I needed a flat piece of tooth structure for modification of the tooth crowns that I was shaping. I glanced over to see if the interpreter was listening. "It's okay, Trudy. I can remove a tiny piece of my own tooth to help shape the molar. We won't have to wait for another donor. It won't hurt me."

Trudy still didn't understand what I was doing, but she acted as if she did. I proceeded as if I knew it was the logical solution to the problem. At first, the men seemed uneasy. They shot a glance at the interpreter, who told them I was just using a piece of my own tooth to help shape the implant.

They bought it. I took my gloves off. While using my dental face mirror, I painlessly flaked off a flat piece of my molar tooth, the right molar tooth! It was the Mikecrodent chip with tooth-colored bonding on it. I carefully placed it in the model teeth to comply with my plan. As I placed the model teeth back into his mouth on the implant abutments, I carefully removed the chip and hid it between my fingers as a magician would. I took a piece of bonding material and rolled it in my fingers like putty and blended the chip into the composite bonding material to make it inconspicuous and laid it aside. I evaluated the bite again, the teeth that opposed the implant teeth.

I got bin Laden to close and open his mouth to adjust his bite and made adjustments to the bite using the lower teeth. I took the Mikecrodent chip, hidden in the mixture of composite bonding putty that I had set aside, and bonded it to the lower molar just as it had been bonded to my tooth. This was his natural tooth and was much less likely to loosen, in the event that that the implants failed, detached from the bone, and subsequently fell out of the mouth. Not this tooth, it was solid, one that I was sure he would keep for a while.

It was at this point that I silently said to myself, *I've got you, you evil villain*. Then suddenly I realized that the prophecy, which was prophesied over me years earlier, had come to pass. I remembered the words so clearly, "Just as David in the Bible conquered the giant with the power of God, so would I." I had just placed a microchip in bin Laden's tooth. Symbolically, he and the other radical Muslim murderers were "The Giants," and I had just slung the first stone from my "sling of tactics." My heart was racing, as I realized that all along God had been preparing me for this moment. That revelation reassured my faith that God would carry out the rest of His master plan. I suspected that the placing of the GPS microchip into bin Laden's body would lead to the striking, the fall, and the removal of the head of "The Giant," once and for all. I pondered in thought for a few seconds and wanted just to bathe in the monumental moment for a few seconds longer, but there was no time for meditation now. Bin Laden's men were watching me closely while I processed these thoughts. I had to get back to the clinical side of things and focus on being a doctor again. I had to appear to the bystanders that my full attention was to provide skillful treatment to the "giant," meanwhile preparing him to take the fatal blow with the symbolic "stone" right in the face, literally. *Only this time, however,* I thought, *the "stone" is going to hit him in his tooth, not between his eyes.* Nevertheless, I thought it would get the job done.

As soon as I had finished adjusting his bite with my naked fingers in his mouth, I scraped his anesthetized tissue, deeply embedding his blood and flesh under my fingernail beds.

I did this to carry back a sample of his DNA, in the event we survived and he was found dead later. DNA sampling might be the only way to verify his remains.

I also was able to obtain some of bin Laden's hair while I was treating him. Two facial hairs had stuck to my gloves during treatment, and I had removed them and placed them next to my instruments, my working area. Looking like I was scratching my armpit, I carefully placed the hair strands under my arm until they took us back to our holding place. I then took the hair strands and wove them into my hair and

Trudy's also, just in case one of us didn't make it back. My goal was to transport samples of bin Laden's DNA back to the United States.

After cementation of the teeth onto the implants, the procedure was complete. The men viewed the replacement teeth, where the once infected and extracted teeth had been, and were finally satisfied. He now had a new set of teeth. But there is no way this procedure would be a success. I had broken every surgical implant protocol in the book, and this one wasn't even in the book. Oh well, they got what they wanted.

Then, it occurred to me. Now that the surgery is over, we have no value. Will they just kill us, or will they wait? My only other option was to convince them that we must continue to monitor the implants. If we didn't, they could fail, and all of this hard work would be lost. There were additional dangers now, from postoperative infection to bone deterioration. I was the only one who would know if his condition started to deteriorate. I told them I had to screen for infection and swelling every three to four hours. They bought this idea or seemed to agree to it temporarily. It provided only a modicum of relief. If they had planned to release us, I had sabotaged the possibility that they would let us go at all. Now, would they even consider releasing us on the outside chance they would need us later? I started to tell them that Trudy had nursing training and would be available to help them with other medical needs, but I hesitated long enough to realize I might be putting her life in danger. If she tried to help someone, and the person died, they would surely kill her. I kept this information to myself.

After we completed bin Laden's surgery, they took us back to our room. As soon as we were alone, I told Trudy what I had done. I had laid the plan that could bring down the giant. The stone of David was my own microchip locator system. She didn't know what to think about it at the time. I don't think she cared. All she cared about were our lives and seeing our kids again.

I felt a sense of accomplishment and was proud that I had successfully performed the surgery to everyone's satisfaction even if it did involve a deceitful and cunning action on my part. I said to Trudy, "What a day at the office. If (and then I corrected myself)...I mean...*after* we survive this ordeal, I'll never consider another 'stressed' day at the office ever again in my life." She didn't think that the comment was funny. I began to second-guess myself and questioned what would happen if the patient were to bite down on something that night and the implants dislodged and came out. I knew that the failure of the surgery would infuriate the men and could come back to haunt us. I quickly focused my mind and concentrated on thinking positive. I remembered having seen cases where I thought there was practically no possibility of success, only to find that the cases had healed successfully. It reminded me of the Scripture, "All things are possible with God." I began to silently pray for healing of the surgical wound and that the surgery would have a successful outcome. I was hopeful that the al-Qaeda men would continue to depend on our abilities and need us for follow-up care. It appeared to me that we were still alive because we were still needed for our skills.

I went over to the sleeping pallet and told Trudy that I was going to take a nap. She said, "How could you sleep now?" I replied, "Jesus went to sleep in the boat while in a terrible storm on the Sea of Galilee, and so am I." I was finally at peace. I slept for about five hours. I knew in my heart that God would bring us out of this situation alive.

I awoke with a horrible sense of dread gnawing at me. For a moment, I thought about my Mikecrodent chip. It was currently in bin Laden's mouth. Even if someone did attempt to locate Trudy and me, they would not find us now. They would find bin Laden. If he were in the same location as we were and the United States forces chose to bomb the underground bunker, we would be killed. My brother was the only one who had any chance of breaking the code and activating the GPS tracking system. I couldn't think straight. I was disoriented and confused.

The strain was beginning to affect Trudy. She was always an optimist, kind, and gentle with my feelings even when I wasn't always the sensitive male. Her tone was harsh and accusatory. She only half listened to me the night before. I knew something was wrong with her.

With a decent night's sleep, I was able to think straight again. I surveyed the room more closely for a way out. The door lock was not that complicated. I removed the orthodontic wire bar from the tongue side of my lower teeth and constructed a handmade lock pick. I bent it in the form of a locksmith pick by sticking it in between the crevices of the rock floor and twisting it to form. I worked for hours on the lock but couldn't get it to turn. The wire was too soft and would bend every time I tried to turn it like a key.

~ 19 ~

The Rescue

We were filthy and smelled of urine. Our hair was matted and filled with trash and bits of straw from the sleeping mats. I was growing a stubby, uneven beard and mustache. My mouth was so dry that my lips were sticking to my teeth. The slimy, nasty taste nauseated me. My throat was parched, and my head pounded with each heartbeat. Trudy's condition was worse than mine. She became tired, restless, and uncommunicative. I was worried about her. I fully expected we would eventually begin to break down physically from the strain we had been under, but Trudy looked weak and sick.

Many hours passed. No one came to give us food. We had only a few ounces of water left in the filthy containers strewn on the floor in the corner of the room. We were very hungry. Every day I beat on the door for about an hour, but no one responded. We had no way to determine the time of day or night. I beat on the door again, and again, but no one came. I began to suspect we had been left alone to die in the dungeon far out in the desert. We were dehydrated and lethargic. I began looking for insects that we could eat. I would consume anything in order to survive. I covered every square inch, for about an hour. I found absolutely no horseflies, no roaches—nothing. We had terrible headaches as we often did when we would fast for days. We had experience in fasting for as long as a week without any food. However, when we did fast, at least we had water. Without water, we would soon die from dehydration.

As Trudy and I lay there on the floor, our bodies grew weaker. Trudy was unresponsive. I was unable to move. In the dark stillness of this underground tomb, I began to pray.

Several soft booming noises began reverberating throughout the building. They were loud enough to bring me temporarily out of my fog. I would soon doze off again. I thought God was opening the floor for us so we could escape.

While in a stupor of a seemingly distant and dreamlike state, I thought I heard thunder and could feel the rock tremble. At first, I thought it might be an earthquake. And then, I thought I was delusional and hallucinating from the slow death of dehydration. A few minutes later, I went off into another sleep state. Shortly afterwards, I awoke to the booming sounds of multiple explosions. The building was vibrating. Then, all hell broke loose around us. Trudy was still sleeping. When I tried to wake her up, she just lay there. I tried to drag her over to the corner of the room where it would be safer if the building collapsed, but I was too weak to pick her up.

As I lay there in total humility, I began to search my spirit, my heart, to evaluate myself and ensure that I was ready to die. I remembered that God's Word told me that "greater is He that is in me than he that is in the world." I reevaluated my calling to missions and my purpose for being there. I knew that much had been accomplished in my life. Not by my own power or might, but by the Holy Spirit. It was the Holy Spirit who led me into the mission field where thousands of people were introduced to the love of Jesus for the first time in their lives.

I knew that the Holy Spirit was with Trudy and me in this prison, and I knew that I was to keep and protect my faith in Him and trust that His will be done over my own will. I would have done just about anything to get Trudy and me out of there unharmed. I knew for sure that I had been sent to Jordan on a mission assignment from God, and that this was where I was supposed to be. However, I didn't understand why all of the punishment and imprisonment was taking place. I questioned why Trudy and I had to endure the pain and torture of all of this hate and madness. And then, I realized that Jesus had been hated and tortured much worse than we had been, and that we were suffering in His name for a purpose. This revelation gave me peace and hope that He was coming for me. None of the material things mattered anymore. It was about Him and me, and my relationship with Him. After I cleared my conscience about my purpose for being there, to advance His kingdom, I began to feel sad about my family. Who would care for them, and what would they ever know of our whereabouts, and how we died? I knew that God would provide for them, as He had done for Trudy and me. I started praying in the Spirit and prayed until I went off into another deep sleep.

Then, suddenly, there was a terrible explosion, so overwhelming that it knocked me unconscious for a few seconds. Rocks and debris were flying everywhere. I wanted to see if the flying debris had injured Trudy, but I was paralyzed from my weakness, unable to move toward her. I was down to my last molecule of energy to survive. I remember the smell of rock dust and gunpowder. It was surprisingly and refreshingly different from what I had been used to smelling down there for so long. It was a new smell and stimulated my thought process. And then I remembered looking up and suddenly seeing a soldier with an American Marine uniform, a radio headset, and a gun pointed at me. His face was not Arabian. He looked American. It was an American face, one that I will never forget. At first, he yelled at us. We were almost unrecognizable as Americans. When I spoke to him and identified myself, he dropped his rifle and said, "We've been looking for you."

I cried. I continued to cry for several minutes as they uncovered us. Trudy was unconscious. I was unable to maintain my focus, but I felt the IV going into my vein. The pain was intense, but it didn't bother me. It meant that I was alive, that I was found, and that someone was caring for me. I let go, finally, and passed out. The next thing I remember was being in a medic helicopter with Trudy by my side. She was unconscious when I tried to talk to her. I tried to ask the medics about her condition, but they just said, "Your wife will be okay, Ray."

I pointed to my hand and tried to make them understand. I had bin Laden's DNA under my fingernail. The medic thought I was becoming agitated and gave me what I assumed was a sedative. I didn't have the energy to fight or explain to him. When we reached the hospital, I scribbled a message on my palm with an ink pen that I took from one of the medics.

The nurse understood and saved the tissue under my nail beds. They also cut my nails and placed them in a sterile bag for evidence. I didn't remember when they cut my nails or when they decontaminated us. At first, she thought I was crazy and delusional, but the military MD deciphered the message on my palm and ordered her to fulfill my written request, just in case that the information might prove significant. At that time, I couldn't talk due to a gastro-estuation tube in my throat, since I had head trauma from the blast during the invasion rescue. Afterwards, they showed me a photograph of the message in my palm that I had tried to write, but could not finish due to fatigue and panic. The incomplete message, only a few words, read, "BL DNA under fingernail, we were..."

~ 20 ~

The Location and Capture of bin Laden

Three days passed before I had strength enough to walk unassisted. Trudy, on the other hand, had kidney failure and needed to have a transplant soon. She was recovering, but her progress was slow. The family all came in to see her, and it was the best medicine she could have received. During the second day of my recovery, I couldn't remember very many details about our ordeal, but I knew that we had been kidnapped and then rescued by the military.

Four days into my hospitalization, I felt that I had to get out of there, and get home. I felt that I had a lot of responsibilities to take care of, since Trudy was still in recovery and unable to tend to her usual pile of lists of things that had to be done. I wanted to get myself together and get back to business as usual to keep the bills from piling up, so Trudy and I could get on with our lives once she recovered and was released from the hospital. We were together for another day, and then my memory began to come back to some degree.

I told Trudy that I needed to call the CIA and inform them that al-Qaeda knew the location of our family. I was concerned because I knew the enemy was still nearby. My family was in danger. I had no way of knowing if bin Laden had called his men off because I had saved his life, or would they be back?

I called the CIA and told them about the spies, and about my concerns for the safety of my family. Agent Roger

Cooper, the CIA director, placed guards around our house. I didn't want to give him the information about the Mikecrodent system over the phone, so I set up an appointment to talk with them the next day. I was overwhelmed with excitement because I knew we were going to finally capture bin Laden.

I had apparently given him enough information to convince him I knew enough to warrant further investigation. Agent Cooper sent a helicopter to pick me up. As the police arrived to watch my family, I was whisked off to headquarters. Agents Satterfield and Weldon briefed me while en route. Satterfield said, "We are taking your family for protection. You will come with us. We have some talking to do." They transported the family to a safe location and flew Trudy to an unknown military hospital for the remainder of her recovery. My goal was to stop a terrorist. My family was in danger and scattered without my presence or protection. This frightened me more than being in captivity in Jordan. I spoke with Agent Cooper over a secured line while in flight, and he assured me that this was the only logical course of action. He said that only a few key agents had knowledge about where my family had been taken. Agent Cooper told me that this was a matter of national security and was "code red-hot, top secret." This comforted me to some degree, and I was able to relax a little and begin talking to Agent Cooper about the secret information.

At this point, the American government didn't know that the Mikecrodent chip had been transferred to bin Laden. During the flight, I told agents Satterfield and Weldon what I could remember. Mainly, the key thing we were talking about was the fact that I got the Mikecrodent chip attached to bin Laden, and we now could locate him. When Agent Cooper discovered this piece of information, he was ecstatic. He immediately called Washington to inform the President. They flew me to CIA headquarters in Langley, Virginia. We were met by a small platoon of Marines.

The two agents and I stayed in the helicopter after it landed while it was towed to a bunker with a large protective concrete covering. Only after the massive protective doors closed behind us did we exit the helicopter. We were immediately taken to the communications center. The building was large and sophisticated. They had everything you could think of when it came to software, hardware, and all in-between.

We opened up the tracking satellite system on one of their computers, but nothing showed up on the monitor. From the time we left to go into Jordan at the beginning of our dental mission trip, I had been recording the tracking device on DVD. Once Agent Cooper discovered this, he immediately ordered a task force to go and get the DVD copy of the recording data for analysis. Within four hours, the task force returned with the recorded DVD data copy and handed it directly to Agent Cooper. How they got it there that fast I don't know, but they did. Agent Cooper handed over the recorded data to Agent Rogers and told him to track the history of the chip's location, from the location where we were rescued. He told Agent Rogers that this information could provide clues as to where some of bin Laden's hiding places were.

Then Agent Cooper told me to activate a live signal, to see if we could locate bin Laden on the monitor. I activated the satellite system and software program, but didn't get a signal. I told the CIA agent that we weren't getting a signal because bin Laden was probably underground, and the rocky terrain blocked the signal. This was confirmed when the analysis of the DVD recording came back. We followed my signal on the DVD when it was attached to me, and to the point where we were captured. They tracked me all the way to the point where we were taken underground. About two kilometers from where the signal stopped, they found us. I pinpointed the location in Saudi Arabia, a town called Sarra, which is about 800 miles east of Jordan.

My brother had gone to the police a week before we were rescued, and told them about the tracking system and said that he didn't know the code. But no one had followed up on it, and the report was still sitting at police headquarters. Even if they had cracked the code, by then the signal would have disappeared. We were already in the underground bunker. The police had no mention of our capture. We were rescued due to the fact that our soldiers had intercepted al-Qaeda radio messages in the location of our rescue, and were sent there on a "kill and destroy" mission. We were very blessed to have survived such a dangerous invasion without being blown up ourselves. They just happened to find us and, at first, thought that we were the enemy. It wasn't until the CIA and the Jordanian government got involved and put the pieces together that they began to know who we were.

I told Agent Cooper that all we had to do is sit and wait until bin Laden came out of his hole, and we would have him. This mission was classified urgent, above top secret, and they quarantined me in a secure room with two guards at all times. It was decided that when bin Laden came out of hiding and started to move and showed up on the tracking satellite, they were to come and get me to help interpret the location and decipher the tracking system. It wasn't until six days later that he came out. They came and got me, and we immediately went to work.

We tracked many signal leads, but would suddenly lose them. They moved above ground for only a short period of time. They would soon return to their vast network of underground tunnels. This went on for quite some time, and then we started to make some progress. It was determined that he was about one kilometer southeast of Riyadh in Saudi Arabia, and the signal began to move fairly fast. Immediately, the Special Forces took charge and went in like a speeding bullet. Bin Laden was there only moments before they arrived, but he disappeared. "Where is he?" we said.

The Special Forces team searched for another two days and still found nothing. He popped up on the screen again, and they quickly invaded the area, where the satellite revealed the location of the chip. They found absolutely no trace of him there. Then, just as fast as he would appear on the screen, he would disappear again. This cat-and-mouse game went on for another ten long, but exciting, hours, until the ground collapsed from underneath one of our military surveillance vehicles, and fell into an underground tunnel, while searching the area. This opened up the ground and allowed the microchip signal to emit. Right away, we picked up the signal and then the captain immediately alerted the Special Forces to move to the target signal location. It was a place called Qatar. The bunker was at Al Wukayr, which was close to Doha. Doha was a small town that harbored an airport and seacoast. The bunker was poorly constructed from aged cement, and the vibrations and weight of the military vehicles proved to be too much for the porous foundation, in the sandy soil, to support. It was there that they found bin Laden with two of his bodyguards. These two turned out to be the two men that were with him when they brought him to me for treatment, back at the medical room during our capture. None of the men survived the surprise attack of the invasion within the tunnel. During their capture, there was a terrible battle of gunfire and explosions. One of the bodies found in the rubble was badly burned by grenades and was identified as Osama bin Laden and confirmed via the DNA that I had obtained from his mouth earlier, and had kept under my nail beds. When I heard of the news, I jumped out of my seat and said, "Yeah—we got him and he ain't no more!"

On the day of discovering bin Laden's body, a vision book was discovered that he kept hidden in his satchel among his apparel. The vision book revealed secret plans that bin

Laden had been working on. It also included key connections with people he worked with to carry out his demands. The book identified his key leaders and appeared to be his form of what we would call his "legal will" which delegated a power of attorney to the next leader in position for command. It described spiritual motives, psychological methods of warfare, military tactics, communication methods, and future plans and directions for al-Qaeda. This book was extremely informative to military officials, which later led to the capture and arrests of many who were involved in terroristic activity. One in particular was the arrest and capture of an American Muslim by the name of Adam Adaahan who had been in more than a dozen al-Qaeda videos calling for the destruction of the U.S. with threats and warnings. He was one of the highest-ranking communication specialists for al-Qaeda.

The United States Armed Forces brought bin Laden's body remains back in a body bag and flew him to the United States with three fighter jets, two Apache helicopters, and two Blackhawk helicopters. After they performed forensic analysis and an autopsy, the body was confirmed again to be bin Laden's. The DNA that was analyzed under my fingernail and from the hair samples that we had collected and brought back matched the body's, which added confirmation to the report. And, to my amazement, he still had the implants in place, and they were still functionally intact. I told Agent Cooper that al-Qaeda had taken my Star of David necklace from me during our abduction, and that I would like to have it back, since it was very special to me. Agent Cooper later told me that the Marines task force, which located bin Laden's body, said that there was significant destruction to the hit site, and that it would be close to impossible to locate such a small item, but that since it was my request, he would do all he could to find it, perhaps with metal detectors. However, my necklace was never located and probably still remains below the rocky surface of the debris. When I told Trudy this, she said,

"Don't worry about it—I'll just get you another one." Once I put perspective on the matter, I just let it go and said, "Okay, but I want one just like the one I had." Trudy just smiled and said, "You've got it. I'll make sure you get your necklace."

~ 21 ~
Meeting the President

Two weeks after the media announced to the world that Osama bin Laden, along with several members of al-Qaeda, had been killed, along with many others being captured and arrested, Trudy and I were invited to the White House to meet the President of the United States and the First Lady. The President wanted to present Trudy and myself with the Gold Cross of Honor, in a recognition ceremony, on-site of the New York Twin Towers, Ground Zero. Of course, we respectfully accepted the invitation, and the event was scheduled.

We were also invited to meet with the President and the First Lady on location at the White House and did so, and talked with them both for about an hour. We talked about our families mostly, and what it was like to be president. We didn't talk much about the mission, except that Trudy told them we were glad to be alive and thanked God for answering our prayers, and that we were so blessed. We had our photographs taken together. I made sure that my new, shiny gold necklace of the Star of David was visible in the photos. I told the President about the necklace, and how Trudy had to get another one for me, since the first one was taken from me. It was a good conversation piece. The President and the First Lady were very kind and gentle. He told me that if we ever needed anything to let his secretary know, since we had a key to the City of New York, as well as to Washington. I told him that there was something I wanted. He asked what it was. I said, "I would like to be exempt from having to pay taxes—for the rest of my life."

They all started laughing and saw that I was serious. He then got serious all of a sudden and said, "I'll see what I can do," and grinned. I didn't know if he was joking or not, but my request was sincere.

I told him that, if it were possible, I would like to have the 9/11 necklace that was found around bin Laden's neck. The President said that he would like to grant me that wish; however, he thought it would be a dangerous item to possess, particularly since there were still radical Muslims throughout the world who would seek out the necklace in memory of their leader's behalf. I responded and said, "You make a good point, Mr. President. You keep the necklace, but I would like to wear it someday just for a moment to symbolize my defeat over him. Only for a moment do I need to place it around my neck, and then I will quickly hand it back over." The President said that he would fulfill my request. I said to him, with a smile, "After I take off the 9/11 necklace, I will immediately replace it with my Star of David necklace."

We all laughed, and Trudy and I were gently escorted to the exit and made our way to the Secret Service helicopter that the President had waiting for us to safely return to our home.

~ 22 ~

The Conclusion

Trudy and I also met with the past mayor of New York City. The media coverage was powerful and provided a small, but incredible element of restoration for our country, which helped start a "sense of closure," at least to some degree, to a traumatic chapter of healing in America.

The Mikecrodent chip got world publicity, and one couldn't imagine how many interviews we were invited to. Larry King, Jay Leno, Barbara Walters—all the big names wanted us. We decided to do just a few of them, and then settle back into our lives again. The mayor of the town in which Trudy and I lived met with the city council, and they decided to name the main hall in the courthouse in honor of me. One of the streets in Washington was named "Trudy Street." Also, there were plans to name a military base after me. There were t-shirts, caps, and bumper stickers about us. And even the American Dental Association awarded me with an honorary membership, and recognized Trudy and me on the front cover of *The Journal of the American Dental Association* that featured our story and the development of the Mikecrodent chip.

It was all so overwhelming! I was amazed at how people saw us as "heroes." But we knew we were just regular people, like anyone else. We had our weaknesses, too. All of the glamour and prestige was nice, but it still wouldn't bring back Carla. It still wouldn't bring back all those people killed in the Twin Towers. It still wouldn't bring back all the soldiers who were killed in combat from fighting the war on terrorism. *What do I do with this heaviness?* I asked myself in deep thought, and I recalled a story about "The Starfish."

It was a story that I heard many years ago about a man that lived on the seacoast. Every morning he would go out and look for starfish that had washed up on the seashore. When he would find one washed up on the beach, he would pick it up and cast it back into the sea again. He did this day after day, every day, as he walked the seashore. One day a neighbor came up to him on the shore, stopped him, and asked him a question: "Excuse me, may I ask you a question?" "Sure," the man said. The neighbor asked, "I live next door to you, and I have noticed for several months now that every morning you come out onto the beach, pick up the starfish that have washed ashore, and cast them back into the sea. Why do you do such a thing, since there are thousands of starfish out here sometimes, and don't you know that, by your doing this, it won't make any difference in saving the starfish, because there are too many of them?"

The man then picked up a starfish at the neighbor's feet, cast it into the sea, and said, "It made a difference to that one."

While meditating on this story in my mind, I concluded that I couldn't always do everything, but I could, at times, do *something*. Although I missed my sister and wanted her back, Trudy and I had created a Mikecrodent locating system to help find missing children, and we were responsible for the capture of the most wanted man in the 21st century. This realization helped me believe that we had made a difference, and that we would continue to make a difference, everywhere we went, from that day forward.

The little things now meant so much more to me. For example, I told my friend Lee, when I saw him shortly after our return, that something as simple as water meant a lot to me, and that if he really wanted to know and appreciate the smooth quality flavor and feel of wet, clean water going down his throat, and down into his stomach, then to just be without it for three days. Then, when he drank it, he would definitely taste it with a different perspective.

I said, "To know you are drinking pure, clean water without the worry of contamination is wonderful. And to take a hot shower and feel clean can only be truly valued when you are without it for two weeks. It is an experience that makes your whole day. Just having fresh water to drink and a hot shower when you feel dirty. It doesn't get any better than that. Or, when you eat cold, dirty rice and chicken with horseflies on it, because you have to in order to survive, and do it for weeks, then a hot American hamburger with mustard and fries makes the world stop for seven minutes. Brushing your teeth for the first time after sixteen days — what a cleansing and refreshing enlightenment. To sleep in a soft, clean, safe, quiet, and peaceful bed, without the worry of sudden unexpected horrors that are real and not mere nightmares. What a splendor to listen to quality music after weeks of silence and Arabic gibber-jabbering! Plus, being free to come and go wherever and whenever you desire is a treasure that I hope I'll never take for granted again. And the most important thing of all, the thing that kept us alive in hope and comforted me in my darkest nights — my faith. God is *everything*. The freedom to worship the true living God, who is full of love, peace, and mercy. That is the pinnacle of the word 'gift.' We are so very blessed. Yes, now I am living the good life. **Thank You, God.**"

Now, as I meditate on the future course of our lives, I ask God in prayer, *What's next?* I am still waiting for the answer.

~ The End ~